THE COWARD WHO DIED ONCE

BY STEPHEN UZOMA OBINNA

authorHOUSE®

AuthorHouse™
1663 Liberty Drive
Bloomington, IN 47403
www.authorhouse.com
Phone: 1 (800) 839-8640

The information presented in this report solely and fully represents the views of the author as of the date of publication. Any omission or potential misrepresentation of any individual or companies is entirely unintentional. As a result of changing information, conditions or contexts, this author reserves the right to alter content at his sole discretion.

The report is for informational purposes only, and while every attempt has been made to verify the information contained herein, the author assumes no responsibility for errors, inaccuracies, and omissions. Each person has unique needs, and this book cannot take these individual differences into account. For ease of use, all links in this report are redirected through this link to facilitate any future changes and minimize dead links.

Published by AuthorHouse 09/16/2019

ISBN: 978-1-7283-2762-4 (sc)
ISBN: 978-1-7283-2773-0 (hc)
ISBN: 978-1-7283-2761-7 (e)

Library of Congress Control Number: 2019914318

Print information available on the last page.

Any people depicted in stock imagery provided by Getty Images are models, and such images are being used for illustrative purposes only. Certain stock imagery © *Getty Images.*

This book is printed on acid-free paper.

Table of Contents

CHAPTER ONE

I could try to convince you that none of this was my fault. Seriously! I had no idea that any of this would happen and that anyone would die. But I've got to admit; I liked the idea of wiping Joe off the face of the earth. His real name was Lewis, however no one called him anything, but Joe. In middle school, he was always screwing around, punching other dudes. Lots of dudes got in fights. But the thing with Joe; you could tell he really liked it when someone got hurt. By high school, he started picking on dudes one at a time. Last year, Joe and his friends destroyed a kid so bad that he quit school. This year, it was me.

I guess I should start from the beginning. It was at the start of 10th Grade at Oak Ridge High School. Joe came back from vacation all bulked up. He looked as though he spent the entire summer in a gym, lifting, and taking roids. Maybe he did. It would explain a lot. It didn't help that he was older than just about everyone else too. His parents had held him a grade, way back when he started grammar school, to give him an advantage over other kids. But holding Joe back didn't do much for him; it only made him bigger than everyone else. The same thing happened to his friend, Greg. And that was probably why they were such good buddies and all.

At the beginning of 10th Grade, I was 15. Joe was 16, but was about six inches taller and weighed 40 pounds more. Greg was 16 and was just as tall, except that he was skinny and more stupid, if that is possible. Zack, Joe's other good friend, was my age. Zack wasn't really dumb like Joe or Greg but he tried so hard to be like them because he thought they were badass and so he might as well be.

At first, it was pushing and shoving and bad-mouthing. My idea was, stay out of Joe's way. That didn't work. I only had one class with him. But after that, we still met at the gym. Even if Joe messed with me there, bad enough that I looked beat up, he always had the excuse he was playing too hard. He wouldn't let me by without a shove. Or, if no one was looking, a punch. It grew worse. Each time, he'd hit harder than the last. Everyone saw what was going on, and painfully, it made all the people I thought were my friends avoid me. Like, they figured, Joe would turn on them too.

I tried getting our gym coach to help. Coach Johnson sat us down and pointed out the fact that we had a problem and advised that we should learn to get along. However, I wasn't the problem, Joe was. And why couldn't Coach see that? The truth is Joe was good at not getting caught, so it was my word against his. All through our discussion with Coach Johnson, Joe smiled. I could tell he was gonna pay me back good. He did.

Finally, I told my dad. "Hit him back!" he said. Dad was probably right that the only thing that would ever stop Joe was if he lost a fight. But I would have to be lucky to win the bout. So, I went back to avoiding him.

On the contrary, that ended up drawing him closer. He knew where I lived: everyone knew where everyone else lived. We had all grown up together. And so, when he couldn't find me at school, he started watching my house. Joe had a big advantage: he had a car. I didn't. His dad had bought him a Mustang GT. Lime green. I have to admit, the car was cool. Any car was cool when you're in high school. No one else in our class had a car except Greg who was even old enough to drive. You'd think having the car would make Joe feel good enough about himself and wouldn't need to bully anyone. All it did was make him more of a jerk.

Now, here's where everything got worse. It was a Monday morning, about a month into the school year. I was walking down the street to the bus stop when I heard Joe's car. I didn't have to turn my head to know who it was. By now, I knew how a Mustang GT sounds. Right away, I started getting this sick feeling in my stomach. The bus stop was about two blocks from my house. I had learnt to time it so I get there right when the bus does. That way, I wouldn't be standing around when Joe drives by and he couldn't yell stuff at me in front of other dudes.

But today, I was late; it didn't look like I was gonna make it. Thinking about Joe made me not want to go to school at all. Every morning, I had to drag myself out of the house at the last possible moment. The only reason I decide to go is because the school would call when you're not there, and that would happen when Dad is at home sleeping, after being awake for, like, days. A pilot, he flies to Japan often. It was his main route. The flights were way long and he always had to sleep a lot afterwards. So, I figured he would be quite furious with me for skipping school if they called and woke him up.

"Hey, freak!"

It was Joe, all right. I didn't turn around; that's the worst thing you could do. I was still half a block away from the bus stop when he pulled up alongside.

"Hey, loser!" he yelled. "Wanna ride? Hey, Zack, should we give him a ride?"

"Naw, losers take the bus," said Zack.

I heard Joe laughing. He has this snorting sound that was really gross. He drove alongside for a few feet as I kept walking. I tried my best to ignore him. As I passed the last house, he swerved suddenly into the driveway, nearly hitting me. Joe, Zack and Greg burst into laughter. You would have thought it was the funniest thing they had ever seen. I felt like killing them all.

"Screw off, dickhead!" I yelled. I have to admit, I was completely crazed. Joe was few steps from running into me; it was practically a miracle he missed me. Had he stepped out of the car right then and there, I would have probably tried to punch him, no matter how much bigger he was. That was how mad I was.

"Make me puke," said Joe.

Just then, I saw the bus barreling down the street. I started racing toward the bus stop. I thought to myself, I'm gonna make the bus after all and it's gonna get me away from this maniac bastard.

But Joe wasn't done with me. As I ran, he swooped in closer, playing chicken as I crossed the street.

It dawned on me I could have proof. I grabbed my cell phone from my pocket and started taking a video. At first, Joe didn't see what I was doing. He was too busy trying to scare the crap out of me as he swerved this way and that way. Then he saw me recording. His face immediately filled with rage. It was kind of frightening how he could go from laughing his head off to sheer fury in about five seconds.

"You shit! You're dead!" Joe said. "You're dead, O'Keefe!"

I believed him. If there wasn't a bunch of people at the bus stop watching, I bet he would have run me over. The worst part was, the moment I got on the bus and looked at the video, I saw that I didn't get anything. There was Joe's Mustang GT, all right, but you couldn't even tell he was the one driving. The car was sort of turning sharply and I wasn't in the picture because I was the one taking it. You couldn't actually tell that he was trying to hit someone. All I had was a few seconds of his car kind of veering. I had been running, hence the picture was unsteady. I was completely disgusted. Now, Joe would try to kill me and it would be for nothing.

CHAPTER TWO

On the bus, following the near-death episode, I realized that no one sat near me. Everyone getting on would see the empty seat next to me and walk past. Then the dude in the row behind me got up and moved to another seat. Dudes were sitting as far away from me as they could, like I was contagious or something. I knew it was because of Joe. I couldn't help obsessing about how much I hated him.

I understood why Joe saw me as someone he'd like to stomp. When 10th Grade started, all the clothes I was wearing were black. My hair was real long because Mom wasn't home anymore to tell me what to do. She and my dad finally realized they weren't gonna get any happier staying together, so she moved out. At least, the yelling stopped. The problem with my dad? He was really wound up tight. Being a pilot and all, he was crazy about being responsible. His excuse was that people's lives were at stake. Mom liked to kick back and have fun. But dad just never relaxed. Never.

Now, you're wondering, what has all this got to do with Joe? See, even though Joe was stupid, he didn't have to be a genius to notice how messed up I was when school started. He must have taken one look at me and figured, yeah, that's who I'm gonna go after. He had found his target and nothing was gonna stop him.

I got off the bus. My first class was algebra. I tried to hand in homework but no one was willing to take it from me. I had to walk all the way to the teacher's desk at the front of the class, which was really embarrassing. I kept wondering if all this was because of Joe. I kind of shrugged it off. But still, it was a little strange. I was half way to the front of the class before I heard what the teacher was saying. When I finally tuned in, I realized we'd been asked to go home and figure it out by ourselves.

The next class was English. I worried all through because gym would follow. I thought about what Joe would do. He was gonna do something, that was for sure. While in class, we were given an assignment that required us to work in groups. But no one wanted me in theirs. This had to be because of Joe, yet I didn't know how. The other kids pushed their chairs together so I couldn't join, while the rest completely ignored me. Finally, the teacher, Mrs. Brown, walked up to me.

"Jimmy? Are you with us today?"

Like it was my goddamn fault no one would let me in their stupid group. That made me upset. But now that she was watching, the other kids had to let me into a group. Only, once she leaves, no one would talk to me. But I couldn't even think about it. I had started to worry about seeing Joe in gym class and I was getting really nervous.

My plan was to get to the locker room late, so that Joe wouldn't be there when I change into my gym clothes. There was something really creepy about the thought of being around Joe when I didn't have any clothes on. I got to the field and put on my shoes. Just then, I saw Coach Johnson with his clipboard. He always held one. I wondered what was on it, since I never saw him write anything down.

"O'Keefe!" Coach Johnson screamed. He never talked in a normal voice if he could scream. He was not a bad person; he just has the idea that the louder he talked, the more important what he said was. This was dumb because no way was Coach gonna say anything that you would need to know in your entire life. He would be telling you to pick up this ball or run that way or go to the locker room or that you're late. As far as I know, he had never even taught anyone how to play any kind of game better.

"O'Keefe, you're late!"

The best thing is not to say anything back. You don't want to start a conversation with Coach Johnson. Someone else was sure to catch his attention if you didn't say anything, and then he would forget that there was ever something he meant to tell you. Out of the corner of my eye, I saw Joe. He was with Zack and Greg. He was watching, so he could enjoy anything bad that might happen to me.

But what caught Coach's attention were two dudes who were a lot late than I was. He was gonna make them pay for it. He was gonna make the whole class pay. He blew his whistle loud. "Around the track twice! That's two times!"

The track was this big loop around the football field. Twice around was a pretty cruel punishment if you were actually running. I saw Joe hanging back, so I took off fast to avoid him. I figured he wasn't actually gonna run if he didn't have to. But it was the twice around that screwed me up. I lost track of Joe. When I didn't see him, I assumed he was behind me. Too late, I saw him hanging out with Zack and Greg at the far side of the loop, as far from Coach as possible. Waiting. I would have to turn and run the wrong way against everyone not to pass by him. I slowed down, not knowing what to do. Finally, I tried to sprint past.

Only, as I did, Zack and Greg formed this kind of shield so Coach couldn't see me. I tried to lose them, but I was running out of breath. Joe picked up speed and I heard Zack say, "Dead man running," and Greg's stupid high-pitched giggle. Then, when Joe was right behind me, he fell intentionally and took me with him.

I went down hard and Joe took the opportunity to slam my face into the track. "You show anyone that video, you're dead," he said.

Here was where I got pissed, because, of course, I couldn't show anyone the video. There was no damned video. Joe didn't know that, and he was just gonna think I wimped out when I didn't. As Joe was getting to his feet, I lost it. I jumped up and hit him as hard as I could. Instantly, I realized how stupid it was to fight Joe when Greg and Zack were standing there. He would want to show off in front of them. He punched me in the face. As I went down, he slugged me in the stomach twice. It was the worst he had ever hit me. It hurt like hell. I couldn't breathe right away.

Across the field, Coach Johnson was looking at his stupid clipboard. He hadn't seen a thing. A couple other dudes saw what had happened and were kind of shocked. They took one look at Joe but didn't do anything. Then Joe and his friends took off like nothing ever happened. Nothing at all.

CHAPTER THREE

I tried to clean up in the locker room after Joe's smackdown but it was useless. The bruise on my cheek was already turning blue. Yeah, it would look terrific in a few hours. I would need to explain everything to Dad, and that meant getting into an argument. He wouldn't understand what I was going through. He couldn't.

I was pretty sure Joe wasn't hanging around. I left the gym and headed to the cafeteria. I paid for my food and walked over to where I saw my friend, Jake, sitting at a table. He was not such a great friend, if you want to know the truth. He kind of pissed me off most of the time because he was into his computer crap and wouldn't answer texts or the phone once he was 'wired in.' It was as if he was cooking up some super secret start-up that was gonna make him richer than anyone else on the planet. The fact is, I knew almost as much about computers as Jake did, but didn't go bragging about it.

Jake didn't even look at me as I walked toward him. He was looking down at his lunch like it was incredibly interesting. That was bullshit because the food in our cafeteria sucked. When I did sit down, Jake, this dude I had known since about the first grade, started piling his lunch items back on his tray.

"Dude," said Jake, "I don't know why Joe is on your case but leave me out of it. Anyone who talks to you, sits near you at lunch, or is friends with you, is next."

I didn't have to ask what that meant and Jake wouldn't tell me even if I had asked. That would mean talking to me. He got up and left me sitting at the table. I felt like a goddamn idiot. All the other tables were filled. But the table where I sat was empty, except for me. I wondered how Joe got the word to everyone so fast. Then it hit me. It was Jake, of course, with his goddamn Facebook alerts and Twitter feeds. Jake was real cagey, wording stuff so no one who wasn't our age would know what he was talking about. Yeah, Joe would've scared Jake into doing it.

I pulled out my phone and clicked on Facebook to see if I was right. I freaked. Like, practically everyone I knew had unfriended me. The only dudes who hadn't were few kids who didn't know Joe because they didn't go to Oak Ridge. El Dorado Hills, the suburb where I lived, was small. We had only one high school.

I was still thinking how much I hated my life when Maddy and her friend, Katrina, sat down a couple of seats away. I didn't immediately recognise who they were. I was staring at my phone and thinking about how much everything sucked. But I got a shocker when they started talking.

"You can't tell anyone," said Maddy. "Why?" asked Katrina.

"Promise."

"Ok."

I looked up and saw this really pretty girl dressed in black, like I was, but not in a depressing way. She wore a black sweater and black skinny jeans. She was hot. You could tell because her clothes were really tight. Her hair was long and jet black, like it had been dyed, but it didn't look phony or anything. I'm explaining all this because if you didn't understand that Maddy was so good looking, you wouldn't believe she did everything she ended up doing. Katrina wasn't nearly as cute.

11

Maddy had this little black velvet pouch that had a symbol, a five-pointed star inside a circle. She pulled out what looked like wax and some black-tipped pins. "I found this cool website all about casting spells," she said, as if her friend should be all impressed.

Katrina didn't look like it was any big deal. "This is wax." Maddy had to explain. "You make it look like the person you're casting a spell on. Then you say stuff." "Oh, my God, what if your mom finds it?"

Maddy smiled. "My mom's not gonna find it. It's gonna find her." You could tell, Maddy was pissed that Katrina wasn't all that impressed. That was the moment she caught me looking at her. I didn't have time to look away. She didn't seem to mind that I had been watching her. In fact, she smiled at me. The truth is, I got everything she said. She was gonna cast some weird spell on her mom. I thought it was pretty strange someone would want to do that.

I was kind of staring at Maddy when she leaned over to me and said, "Cool shirt." She got up and walked off. Katrina followed.

I looked down and noticed that I was wearing my black skull tee shirt. It was a black skull on a black shirt, so you couldn't make out the skull unless you were really up close. It was cool. Teachers couldn't freak and send you home since they couldn't see it. It was like everything else at the screwed-up school; they had a screwed-up dress code.

Maddy liking my shirt made me forget how insane it was that she wanted to put a witch's spell on her mom. That was too bad. I should've known right then and there how messed up she was and stayed away from her.

CHAPTER FOUR

J ust like I thought, Dad and I got into an argument because of Joe. I was in my room trying to do the algebra I missed in class. It sucked that I couldn't call anyone for help. I figured no one would answer the phone if they saw it was me. It didn't help that my face was hurting. It made me think over and over about getting slammed by Joe and how other dudes saw it and didn't say anything. The only way I could focus was by putting on headphones and playing Imagine Dragons insanely loud. That way, I didn't hear Dad when he got home. I guessed he had called me or something and I hadn't answered. He barged into my room like he was all mad. But before he could say anything, he noticed I was all beat up and stood, staring at me.

"You asked me to hit him back," I admitted. I wanted him to feel guilty, so he would finally agree to get me out of the damn school.

Dad kept looking at my face. "Did you report this?" "And get suspended for fighting?"

"If he attacked you..."

"Right. That's just what he'll say."

"Where are all the teachers at that school?"

I just shrugged. Dad seemed to believe there was some kind of solution out there, some rational solution.

"I'm going to talk to the principal." "Dad, I need to get out of there."

But he wasn't listening. "It's the best school in the district. I bought this house so you could go to that school. I bought out your mother's share of this house so you could keep going to that school."

I lost it. "Dad, please! Just get me out of there!"

Then he came up with an even worse plan. "I'll call his father." Yeah, that would make Joe love me. Why couldn't my dad see that his ideas were crap? "His father is just like him."

Dad became very tense. When he is tense, his voice is quiet. "Then if you're going to hit back, hit back harder."

I got real sarcastic and said, completely deadpan, "Oh, that's the answer. Thanks, Dad."

I could tell Dad felt like I just called him a jerk. I could tell he was pissed but I didn't care. I was hurt and he was not helping me. I pulled my headphones back on and ignored him like he wasn't in the room. You really shouldn't do that with my dad. He's a very proud guy and he gets offended at stuff like that. But I was mad. He stood there for a moment, like he wanted to say something more. Finally, he understood I wasn't going to listen and left.

I decided that if Dad was not gonna help, I would escape Joe by going to live with Mom. I considered calling her and explaining everything. But I figured she would want to talk to Dad. And they'd start arguing. They had a big old argument about where I was gonna live when they divorced. Whenever they argued, Dad always won. This time, I didn't want him to win. I figured it was a better idea if I just showed up with my laptop and a few clothes. Then it would be, like, done.

Mom lived in San Francisco near Golden Gate Park. Her apartment was really small yet she always said she was lucky to get it. I didn't understand why she liked San Francisco so much. Everything was all packed together and there was a ton of people everywhere you looked. I mean, yeah, it was kind of nice that you could drive out to the end of the avenues and see the ocean but where she lived was kind of run down. The paint was even peeling from her apartment building because of the fog. There was always fog and it made everything seem really depressing.

Dad's next flight was to Japan. With stops, it was about hours each way, and there was about a day's layover in-between. The day after he left, I cut school and headed to my mom's. I rode my bike to the station, took the light rail to Sacramento, got on Amtrak to the Bay Area, switched to rapid transit, then caught the streetcar. It took about five hours. I hadn't told Mom I was coming. Like I said, I figured the best thing was just to show up. I started to panic as I got there because I had no idea if she was even at home. But when I rang the bell, she buzzed me right in. As I went up the stairs, I realized I had no idea what I was gonna say. Not that it would have mattered, even if I had a speech all prepared. She gave me this big hug and started firing off questions.

"What are you doing here by yourself? Aren't you supposed to be in school? Where's your father?"

I decided it was best to answer the last one. "Over the Pacific, somewhere."

Immediately, she got suspicious, especially because my face was all bruised. "Is he mistreating you?"

"No. Dad's fine. I just need to live somewhere else right now. Like, really soon. I mean, if that's all right."

For a moment, she didn't say anything. She sank down on the couch. I began to think that maybe it wasn't all right.

"Mom?" This time I waited. She needed to give me an answer.

"Oh, honey," she sighed. "Your dad would fight me. He'd be furious. I can't go through that again."

"Maybe he wouldn't."

"Of course, he would. You're his whole life."

I guessed she didn't want me there. I couldn't believe she wasn't jumping at the chance for me to stay. The fact is, she and my dad did fight for me. Hard. As I tried to figure this out, I saw a pair of men's slippers near the sofa. They were not my dad's. All of a sudden, I figured Mom had a boyfriend. No wonder she didn't want me there. The place was tiny, and there was not even an extra bedroom. I'd hear everything.

"It's OK, I get it. I'd be in the way."

My mom is a really bad liar. "Honey, you're never in the way. But it doesn't make sense to do this now, right in the middle of the school year."

I nodded. As I looked around, I saw the pictures that were in our house before. There was one of Mom and I when I was little. It was like a picture of someone who didn't exist anymore. The pictures and the men's slippers started making me really sad.

I decided I had to leave before I start crying, for God's sake. I picked up my pack and headed for the door. I guessed my mom kind of felt guilty, because she said, "Jimmy? There's nothing really wrong, is there?"

I needed to get out of there fast, so I said, "No. Everything is great."

She didn't buy it but she didn't try to stop me from leaving, either. I walked down the stairs. I felt so sad than I had ever felt in my whole life. As I waited on the sidewalk for the streetcar to take me back, all I could think was, I wouldn't want to live here anyway. I hate the goddamn fog.

I headed back, retracing my route until I was on the light rail heading home. It was the last train and practically deserted. I was dead tired. I dreaded the uphill bike ride back to my house. I had school tomorrow, which was gonna be a pain because I had missed today. And Joe. There was still Joe. I was feeling pretty sorry for myself when my cell phone rang. It was Dad. In a flash, I knew Mom had called him to ask what was wrong with me. That meant he knew I cut school to see her. I bet she woke him up. Now, he'd be mad because he would have to worry about me instead of resting before his flight back.

There wasn't any static on the call. I heard perfectly how angry he was all the way from Japan. I said, "Dad," a few times, trying to get a word in, but he didn't want any excuses. I was supposed to call him no matter what time I got home, so he could stop worrying. That was gonna give him a whole extra chance to chew me out. I didn't even want to think of how long it would take before I got home.

As I hung up, I said, "Shit!" loud enough. You would have heard it, even if you were a few seats away. Someone did and started laughing. It was like a cackle. I turned and saw Maddy. I didn't see her get on. The train had doors front and back. She got up and slid in the seat right beside me. I was stupid enough to think it was cool.

CHAPTER FIVE

"Yeah, parents suck. I'm Maddy. I'm in the class behind yours."

I couldn't help but stare at her. She was so pretty. Same as before, she wore a tight sweater. But this was sky blue, same color as her eyes. She wore this black makeup that made her eyes seem huge. She was looking right at me. It took a moment before I could even think of something to say. Finally, I managed, "I'm Jimmy. You liked my shirt."

"I know who you are. You're Jimmy O'Keefe. You're that guy no one is supposed to talk to."

"How come you're talking to me?" "Maybe I'm not like everyone else."

Maybe she wasn't, I thought. I remembered she was discussing with her friend about casting spells. I didn't know anyone else who did stuff like that. "What happened with your spell?" I asked.

Maddy was not the least embarrassed. "Oh, you heard that. It didn't work. I made this little wax doll. It looked just like my mom. I even used strands from her hairbrush. It helps if you use something that actually belongs to the person. Then I lit this black candle so I could read the chant. It's better if you do it in the dark. Don't ask me why. The chant is the Lord's Prayer backwards. I know it forwards. Of course, everybody does. But not backwards. Did you know saying the Lord's Prayer backwards is really, really a powerful spell? Maybe you should put a curse on that guy who hates you. What's his stupid name?"

"Joe."

"Anyway, the candle wax dripped all over and the doll's hair started to burn. It smelled awful. The next thing I knew, my mom was banging on my bedroom door. Oh, my God, she was screaming the whole time to let her in. I just managed to hide everything before she kicked in the door. Of course, she knew I was doing something, so she had to scream at me for, like, an hour. She screams when she's drunk, which is practically every night. Once she's in my room, I can't shove her out. Believe me, I try, but she's big. At least, she didn't hit me, this time. She would've if she knew what I was doing. But the doll got all messed up, and now I can't get it to look like her anymore."

It was kind of shocking listening to Maddy. The stupid witches' spell was all mixed up with a story that sounded pretty awful if it was true. I didn't know what to think. I mean, I didn't know any moms who got screaming drunk, kicked in doors, and hit kids. A dad, maybe.

Maddy glanced at me. "You don't believe me." She pushed up the sleeve on her sweater and showed off an ugly black and blue mark on her arm. "See? If I showed this to a teacher and said, this happens all the time, they might do something. But oh, my God, here's the thing: they'd just put me in a foster home somewhere. You can end up anywhere. I mean, anywhere. No, she totally has to die. It's no good if she just sickens and wastes away. Uh-uh."

Maddy hastened to add, "Honestly, I don't need her to feel any pain. I'm not that kind of person. A car crash would be fine. I just need her to be gone forever."

I had known Maddy for about five minutes and she was telling me she wanted her mom to die in a car crash. Now, you're wondering, why didn't I jump up and change my seat? Because what she said was too crazy, I didn't really believe she meant it. I didn't want to believe anything that bad about her. She was way too pretty. I just said, "Well, now I know why you liked my shirt."

She giggled and looked at me like she wished I would be in on the joke with her. I admit, I smiled, too. She noticed my stuffed backpack and asked, "Were you running away?"

"No," I said. She kept looking at me like she knew I was lying, so I finally shrugged, "Yeah. I was gonna try to live with my mom. It didn't work."

Maddy noded. "Exactly. That was exactly what I was thinking. I don't have a dad, in case you're wondering. I was gonna run away with my boyfriend. Only, he got freaked. My mom called him and told him he better stay away. She used the R-Word and he freaked out."

The R-Word? I was trying to figure out what she meant without appearing dumb and actually asking.

Maddy sensed my confusion. "The R-Word. He's. I'm."

I got it. I couldn't help it. I just stared at her. Maddy looked back at me and smiled like she understood everything I was thinking, which she probably did. What dude wouldn't be thinking that?

"After he didn't answer my phone calls for, like, a week, I went looking for him at his work today and he told me what she said. I told him, 'OK, Matt, I don't have to come live with you, just help me do something.' But instead of him saying he'd help me, he broke up with me. I am so mad. He's gonna be sorry, you'll see."

"Help you do something?" I asked. I wanted to know what she was talking about; I wanted to nail down if their break-up was gonna stick.

All of a sudden, Maddy went real vague, "Oh, you know."

I didn't get what she meant. I was still trying to figure it out when she cut in, "I hear Joe's going to destroy you."

The second Maddy made that statement, I got bummed again. "Yeah."

"You're just gonna let him?"

"Are you kidding? I'd do anything to get rid of him." "Anything is anything."

"Well, I mean, I can't, like, kill him." Maddy smiled. "Why not?"

"Yeah, right," I said, sarcastically.

The train stopped and most of the other people got off. There was no one sitting near us. Maddy leaned closer, like she was my girlfriend or something.

"If you could get away with it, would you?" she asked. "I'd never get away with it."

"Because everyone would think it was you."

"That's one good reason." "Maybe I could help you."

"Help me? I don't even know you."

"That's why it'd work. No one would know. No one could figure it out."

For a moment, I actually considered what she was saying. It was so crazy; I couldn't help but smile. The idea of Maddy going after Joe was pretty funny, let me tell you.

"See? You like the idea," she said. "Like it could ever happen."

"Oh, it could. 'Course, then you'd owe me."

Maddy looked at me again, like she was in love with me. I was wondering if she was serious or if this was some kind of a joke, when the train started to slow.

"I need to meet my friend. Her mom wants to give me a ride home," Maddy said, as she stood up. "Think about it."

She got off the train. I kept staring out the window until the train moved and I couldn't see her anymore. I didn't tell her I had a bike, so it was kind of mean she didn't ask me if I needed a ride. Then it hit me: maybe she was serious and didn't want anyone to know we had met. Maybe she didn't want anyone to see us together. That was crazy, I concluded.

CHAPTER SIX

I knew the day was gonna be bad. I just didn't know how bad. It started with Jake's warning. I was in the locker room, changing into gym clothes, when I saw Jake looking around to make sure no one else was watching. "Hey! I heard your dad called Joe's dad from China."

I was surprised Jake was even talking to me. He was so scared of Joe. At first, what he said didn't even hit me. "Japan," I replied. "My dad was in Japan."

Jake stared at me like I was a moron. "Do you even get it? Your dad called Joe's dad. You're lunch, dude."

I finally got it. I immediately sat down on the bench and began pulling off my gym shoes, because the one place I knew Joe could find me was the gym. Then Coach Johnson saw me.

"O'Keefe!" he bellowed. "You cut my class yesterday. No one cuts my class!"

"I was sick, Mr. Johnson. And I'm still sick. I need to sit out."
"You got a note?"

I shrugged. Of course, I didn't. "You cut my class, you suffer."

I was so mad; I slammed my locker shut, which was not the smartest thing to do in front of Coach Johnson. He gave me this look like he was gonna write me up. But that would mean writing, so I knew he was just gonna take it out on me in class. He waited around for me to retire my shoes so he could escort me to the gym personally. But when we got there, Coach got distracted by this dude dripping blood all over the precious Oak Ridge basketball floor on account of - he got elbowed in the face by some other dude during a half-court game. That was when I saw Joe glaring like he wanted to kill me.

Joe started moving toward me. Zack and Greg were right behind him. I threw a desperate glance at Coach, but he was leaving with the kid who got hurt. Joe moved in closer and I saw that he had a black eye. I suddenly became really scared.

"Think you're smart? Whack job calling my dad."

Joe didn't wait for an answer. He punched me in the face without any warning and I went down. Then he kicked me once, hard, at the base of my spine. It was a pain I had never felt before. Then, as Greg and Zack huddled close to screen him from Coach Johnson's view, he lifted my head by the hair and pounded my face into the floor.

"He ever gets called again, you're gonna fuckin' die."

No one helped me up. No one. They were all too afraid. I can't recollect how I managed to get back to the locker room and changed out of my gym clothes. My head was ringing. I could barely walk. I thought about going to the principal. But on my way there, I saw Greg and Zack hanging out in front of his office. I turned around and heard them laughing.

I figured I had to put something cold on my face to keep the swelling down. I was panicking that my eye was gonna get all black and blue, 'cause if it did, my dad would freak and call Joe's dad again. I was feeding coins to a vending machine to get a cold can of Powerade when I heard someone speak.

"Again?"

It was Maddy.

I turned away. I wasn't in the mood to talk to anyone at the moment. The truth: it was pretty humiliating to get beat up.

"So, which is it, O'Keefe? Him or you?" I didn't answer.

"Seriously," Maddy said.

"Yeah, right." I said sarcastically. I just wanted her to go away. I held the cold Powerade can to my face. It hurt like hell where it touched. "Ow! Shit!"

"There's only one way to make him stop," Maddy said, but I couldn't hear her clearly. My ears were ringing. She sounded as though she was far away, even though she was standing right beside me.

"Do you want it to stop?" Maddy asked.

I had the can covering my face, so I couldn't even see her. I heard her say again, "Do you want it to stop, O'Keefe?"

I wasn't really thinking anything except that, of course, I wanted it to stop. "Yeah," I answered.

"Then you're in."

I didn't say anything else. For a while, I just stood there, holding the stupid can to my face. Then, finally, when I put the can down, I noticed that Maddy was gone. I was confused, trying to remember what she said.

"What?" I asked. But she wasn't there anymore.

CHAPTER SEVEN

When my dad got home, he slept for a day and a half straight. That was OK with me. I didn't want to talk to him. I didn't want to talk to anyone. I wore headphones whenever I was at the house. I had shut down my Facebook page. And, at school, if I wasn't in class, I would be hiding out in the library. I wrote a note to get out of gym for two weeks and forged my dad's signature. Coach said he wanted to see a note from a doctor, so I put together some phony letterhead on my computer and wrote that, too. My dad woke up and noticed that I had stopped talking to him. He tried to start a conversation but I was too pissed off.

I had not seen Joe for some time. I figured he was laying off for a few days until his dad cooled off. I knew it was only a matter of time before he would try something again. He wouldn't be able to help himself. Bullying was like a goddamn drug for him. I thought to myself, maybe the only thing left for me to do was try to get expelled. I knew just how to make that happen. I was going to need a weapon to overcome Joe's physical advantage, and using a weapon would get me out of Oak Ridge for sure. A stun gun would do nicely, I decided. I was happy about it, knowing that it would pay Joe back with some serious pain. I didn't even do a background check. I knew that it would take some planning to get one, because I didn't want anyone to think my dad had anything to do with it. I figured I would have to order it online. I could lie about my age if I had to.

I didn't want to leave a trail on my own laptop. I was looking up all this stuff on the computer in the school library, when I saw a girl looking at me kind of sorrowfully. She was one of the girls who tutored other kids during lunch. She looked like she wanted to say something. But I didn't want to talk to anyone, especially when I was in the middle of doing something illegal. I pulled up the hood on my sweatshirt; she got the message and left me alone.

That night, my dad sprang his latest. He had got his airline to agree to let him swap his route, so he wouldn't be away so long at a time. Instead of flying international, which was cool, he would be flying domestic. That weekend, I had to go with him. The Oak Ridge homecoming game was Friday night, and I would be on a plane doing homework. He didn't say if it was for less money. But, of course, it was. I guessed my mom made him feel guilty. It made me kind of sad, because I knew Dad loved flying to all those foreign places. On Friday afternoon, I climbed into his Ford Explorer. He looked sternly at my black tee shirt, black hoodie, and black jeans. But he didn't say anything.

I made one last plea. "Do I have to go? There's no point."

"I want to keep you out of trouble until this problem goes away."

Right, I thought, mockingly. Joe was just gonna go away. "Sure, Dad."

Dad started his SUV.

"Where are we going anyway?" I asked. "New York."

I thought of how much that sucked. There was only gonna be enough time to sleep and eat before we would have to head back.

"By the way, I called that kid's father," my dad said. I was completely deadpan. "I heard."

"He won't be bothering you anymore, so no more talk about changing schools."

I could barely keep the scorn out of my voice. "Yeah, it worked, Dad. You don't ever have to call anyone again."

I started searching through my backpack for my headphones. I didn't know how much more of it I could take. But New York wasn't as bad as I thought. After we got to our hotel and slept, I was hungry. Dad took me to a restaurant that had the biggest sandwiches I had ever seen. The waiter thought it was cool how much I could eat. For a few minutes, I just zoned. There was so much space between Joe and I. For once, I could actually breathe. I noticed my dad was looking at me like he wanted to say something. I became scared that he finally noticed the bruise on my cheek. But that was not what he wanted to talk about.

"Your mother," he began. "I don't know what she told you."

I realized he knew about her boyfriend and wanted to make sure I was OK. I shrugged and said, "I guess mom's moving on with her life."

He figured that I already knew and that I was not all freaked out, so he smiled at me. I could tell he was thinking the same thing as I was: it was just us from now on. We didn't say anything else. All of a sudden, we were friends again. Only, now I didn't know if I could go through with my plan to get expelled. My dad really hated guns. He hated all violence. He actually knew one of the pilots on a plane that hit a tower only a few miles from where we were sitting. That made him hate violence even more. I just couldn't do this to him. But I didn't want to start talking about Joe. I was feeling real good because I was having this conversation with my dad and I didn't want goddamn Joe to spoil it. I knew I would have to tell my dad what happened, but I just didn't want to do it then. I didn't want to talk about it in front of a taxi driver either. After that, we were back on the plane.

There was a family in my row. I sat next to a five-year-old kid who was kicking the hell out of the seat in front of him. The man in that seat kept turning around and glaring. The kid didn't stop because no one else was paying him any attention. He saw me watching him and gave me this goony expression. It cracked me up. Instead of finishing my homework, I let him play a game on my laptop and he completely ran out the battery. His mom smiled at me, because for once she didn't have to pay attention to her kid. When we landed, the kid started kicking the seat again because his mom got on her cell phone right away. That reminded me to turn mine on. I was not even thinking I had any messages, since no one had sent me a text in, like, ages. But my phone started going crazy and I saw I had all these texts. When I read the first one, I couldn't help it. I yelled, "HOLY SHIT!" as loud as I could. I started reading the others. Again, all I could do was say, "Holy shit! No way! No fucking way!" over and over. The woman gave me this real dirty look for cursing in front of her kid. But I didn't care.

Joe was dead.

CHAPTER EIGHT

Joe was dead. Some kind of weird accident in his car, only there was nothing in the texts that said how. Somehow, Joe's car caught fire and he was in it. At that moment, I didn't care how. All I knew was, I was happy. I was incredibly happy.

I couldn't wait to tell my dad, but the plane was filled and I was in the row before the last. I had to wait until everyone in the rows ahead got a goddamn huge piece of luggage out of the overhead. Finally, it was my turn. I was in the aisle of the plane at the back of this line of people. As I was getting close to the front, I saw my dad leave the cockpit. Just then, this El Dorado County sheriff's deputy stepped inside. He was saying something to my dad. I noticed Dad looked shocked. Finally, I got close enough to hear my dad say, "My God, that's terrible."

The deputy looked at me. He seemed to know who I was. But instead of talking to me, he kept talking to my dad. "We need to ask your son some questions."

My dad looked puzzled. "Jimmy? Why?"

I was now close enough to read the deputy's name tag: Baker. Deputy Baker said, "According to the boy's father, his son and Jimmy were having problems."

For the first time, I figured that maybe Joe's death wasn't an accident. I stared at the deputy; I couldn't believe it. Then I understood why he was there, even before my dad did.

Dad said, "That got cleared up. I spoke to his father last week."
"Well, no sir. They got into another fight a few days ago."

Dad looked at me in surprise, which made Deputy Baker look at me like I had lied to my father.

"It wasn't a fight," I explained.

Deputy Baker gave this nice, reassuring smile. "Well, sure, let's sit down. We want to hear your side."

But then my dad cut in and said, "Not without a lawyer."

I stared at Dad. I couldn't figure what harm there was in saying Joe beat me up.

Deputy Baker said, "It'd help us out if we could ask some questions."

But Dad was firm: "Not without a lawyer."

Deputy Baker looked annoyed. He knew he wouldn't get anywhere. He pulled out a piece of paper and waved it at my dad. "We have a warrant for your son's computer. Don't worry, he'll get it back."

My computer had all my homework and notes from school. The battery had run out and there was no way to get the stuff I needed. I unziped my pack and handed it to the deputy. I could tell my dad was pissed.

"Where were you when it was my son getting beat up?"

Deputy Baker was probably still annoyed that my dad didn't let me talk to him. He gave Dad a suspicious look. "Sounds like maybe you were angry at this boy as well."

Dad was way too smart to say anything back. He just looked at the deputy stonily, like the deputy was the asshole he was.

Finally, Deputy Baker said, "We'll be in touch," and he left.

My dad turned to me, bewildered. "How could they think you did anything? You were with me all weekend."

"I don't know," I said. And the truth was, I didn't. I didn't even think about Maddy.

At the airport, Dad stopped at the newsstand for a paper. There was a big article about what happened to Joe and he made me read it out loud as we drove home. I couldn't read the whole thing. I had to skip over the parts that talked about what a promising young man Joe was. In the article, they didn't call him Joe, of course; they used his real name, Lewis Nelson. It was strange. It was like reading about someone else, not the person I actually knew.

According to the article: Joe was at the Oak Ridge homecoming game when, for some reason, he left at half- time. None of his friends saw him go. No one could figure out why he left; he was supposed to drive his friends home. The next thing anyone knew, Joe was in his car, which was parked on a road near Folsom Lake, the big lake that bordered El Dorado Hills. The car was on fire and he was inside, all burned up.

The police or the fire department - the article wasn't that clear - found Joe because someone reported the smoke from the burning car. The story said the police were investigating it as a homicide, only they didn't say why they thought so. Also, a big downpour started right around the same time and the evidence that wasn't burned up probably got washed away.

They didn't clearly state that there was no evidence; they just quoted an El Dorado sheriff's deputy who said that evidence had been "degraded." As far as I could tell, no one knew what the hell happened, and maybe they were never gonna find out.

The newspaper didn't say a thing about me.

It was pretty late when we finally got home. I crawled into bed without even eating. I was thinking about how I was gonna explain to my teachers that I didn't have my homework because the El Dorado County sheriff took my computer. I thought of what they were going to say about that. I thought about it for a while, but I was damn tired. I fell asleep.

CHAPTER NINE

It was weird. I was waiting for the bus on Monday and no one was afraid to talk to me anymore. Even dudes who weren't my friends went out of their way to say hello. I don't know how I felt about it. I mean, it was bullshit, really.

When I got off the bus, Zack and Greg were waiting. I had nothing to say to them so I walked right by. But they followed.

At last, Greg said, "We hear your dad won't let you talk to the cops."

I ignored him. But I wondered how Greg knew that. That was before I found out that everything about Joe's death was being reported on the TV news, like Joe was this innocent victim or something. Also, this news guy was reporting that Joe had a problem with someone at school, and that person Joe had the problem with wouldn't say anything. Of course, everyone knew it was me.

Zack said, "Maybe it's 'cause you know something." Greg's voice was all harsh. "We know you hated him." "Everyone knows that," added Zack.

I wasn't gonna let Greg and Zack take over Joe's bullying. So, I turned around to face them straight on, and I leaned in to get right in their faces. "Something else you need to know," I said. "I hate you, too."

They both looked shocked. I couldn't help thinking it was funny as hell because they thought I had anything to do with killing Joe. It was even funnier that it made them scared of me.

At lunch, people were kind of looking at me as I waited in line at the cafeteria. Jake saw me and smiled like he remembered he was my best friend forever or something. I went to sit down and figured he was about to come over. Then I saw Zack watching. Zack never ate lunch in the cafeteria; he and Greg would usually sneak off campus and get fast food.

Sure enough, Jake sat down across from me and the first thing he said was, "So, dude. How did you do it?"

"I didn't."

"You gotta admit, it's kind of strange it happened on the one weekend you were out of town, sitting on an airplane for no reason."

"Dude," I said, "I had nothing to do with it."

Then Jake said, "Yeah, but, y'know, it'd be so cool if you did."

Right then I decided I didn't want to talk to Jake. I grabbed my stuff, and I hoped he got the message; I didn't want to talk about Joe. It was not like I disliked Jake. I remember he tried to warn me and all, but I wasn't going to let him mess with my head. I sat down at an empty table and tried not to notice that everyone was watching me.

And that was when the girl I saw in the library about a week ago walked over. "Hi, I'm Lila. You might think this is crazy," she began.

I was thinking, what now. But then I figured, why not talk to her. She was actually kind of pretty. She was Asian - or maybe part Asian. She had this beautiful hair and a really nice smile. But the thing I noticed about her was that she dressed kind of edgy, like she lived in a city. I had just returned from San Francisco. She could fit in there.

"That's OK. A lot of things are crazy right now," I said. "I want to apologize," she continued.

I was confused. I had never even talked to this girl before. "For what?"

"Everyone was just so mean to you. It was really sad. You looked totally alone."

I wondered if she got what she was saying to me. "So, you came over to tell me I'm pathetic?"

She looked kind of shocked. "I didn't say that." "Actually, you kind of did."

Lila saw that everyone was watching both of us. She looked embarrassed. "Wow. Just forget it."

"I mean, you could've said you wanted to sit here because you didn't think I was pathetic." I got pissed off, got up and walked away.

Immediately, I realized I was acting like a jerk. I remembered she did look like she wanted to talk to me in the library a few days earlier, and that it was my fault she didn't. It was just that, with everything that had happened, it was hard to trust anybody. I looked back, and that was when I saw Maddy at a table across the room. She didn't make the slightest sign she knew me. When she caught me looking at her, she looked away. But I was thinking about this girl, Lila, whom I had just insulted. I wanted to apologize for being mean. I left the cafeteria but I couldn't find her.

Maddy had something to say to me. Only, she didn't want to say it in front of anybody. She didn't want anyone to see us talking. As I walked to the bus after school, all of a sudden, she was beside me. I heard her say in this real quiet voice, "We need to talk."

"Yeah? I mean, sure. What about?"

"Don't play dumb, O'Keefe. Because of me, your life just got a whole lot better."

I remembered what she said about going after Joe. All I could think of at that point was that she thought her little witchy curses had something to do with what happened to him. I was sarcastic as hell when I said, "Yeah, right."

"Want proof?"

There was no way I believed her. So, I said, "Yeah," still totally cynical.

"Not here. I don't want people to see us together," Maddy said. She started walking to the area by the Oak Ridge tennis courts. I thought it was dumb, but I followed her. No one was playing; the courts were empty. She looked around carefully before handing me a brown envelope. She didn't say anything, but just kept looking at me with a funny little smile. I opened the envelope and pulled out what was inside. That was when I freaked: I was holding Joe's driver's license.

"Jesus! JESUS! Are you kidding me? Are you freaking kidding me?" I was so stunned. I fumbled and the license dropped to the ground.

Maddy was smiling like a cat. "He was driving. He had it with him. Not that it actually proves anything, of course, but I think it does."

Suddenly, I thought she could have killed Joe. I didn't know how she did it. But maybe she did. Somehow.

"And now it's yours," Maddy said. She meant Joe's license, like it was some kind of trophy.

"No, I don't want it!" My hands were shaking as I picked up the license and put it back in the envelope.

Maddy grabbed the envelope back from me. "That's cool," she shrugged. "But you know what? You will do what I want. Like I said, you owe me."

"What are you talking about?" "My mom. I hate her."

It took me a few seconds to get what she was saying. And when I did, my heart almost stopped. "I'm not gonna kill someone."

"You don't get it," Maddy said. "You already did."

All I could do was stare after her as she walked away. I saw my bus starting to pull out. It was about a five-mile walk home but I couldn't move. That was when it hit me: I had not even asked her what happened.

I ran up to her. When she saw me, she flared. "Are you retarded? Stay away from me or people will see us."

"How did you do it?" I asked. She looked nervous. She feared someone was going to see me with her, but I didn't care.

"How?"

She knew I wasn't going to believe her until she told me. So, she thought up a place we could meet. This time, as she walked away, I didn't follow.

CHAPTER TEN

I was waiting for Maddy a couple hours later at a park. I was at the far end of a grassy field where little kids were playing T-ball. The kids were young enough. They probably didn't have brothers or sisters my age, so I didn't recognize any of the parents. Maddy had already told me to leave if she did not show up. None of the parents paid me any attention; they were all just watching their own kids. But it made me feel creepy that I was there, watching little kids play T-ball, while I was waiting to find out how someone got murdered.

I started thinking about what was in the newspaper, about no one knowing why Joe left the football game. The paper had this picture of Joe, so everyone could see how big he was, and people would understand that no one could've made Joe leave if he didn't want to. I had an idea how Maddy could've made Joe want to leave. But the rest, I had no clue.

At last, Maddy got to the park. When she was convinced that no one was looking at us, she asked what it was I wanted to know. I said, "Just tell me what happened." I was gonna need a pretty good story to believe her. Maddy started talking. A lot. She had to tell someone how clever she had been and she had no one to tell but me.

"I watch these TV shows," Maddy began. "You know, Datelin, Hours, shows like that. You ever watch them?"

I shook my head. "No. I never watch stuff like that."

"Well, if you did, you'd know they're much better than CSI," Maddy explained. "That's because they're about real murders where someone really murdered someone and then got caught. If someone didn't get caught, they couldn't do a show about it. So, you learn the stupid thing that made someone get caught."

She paused. I figured it was my turn to say something. "So, what stupid thing didn't you do?"

She looked at me like I was dumb. It was so obvious. "I didn't know Joe. I didn't have a motive. The police always look for whoever wanted someone dead, like the husband or the wife, or whoever got the dead person's money."

"Or the dude who got bullied. Hey, thanks." I was back to sarcastic.

"But since you didn't, they can't prove it. By the way, good alibi."

She said this like I planned it, and that made me go nuts. "Joe," I said, to remind her what we were there to talk about.

"I knew getting him to go somewhere with me wouldn't be hard." Maddy smiled and I nodded. I already got that. "But getting him to go without his dumb friends seeing or without him telling them about me, that was the hard part. Because he had these friends he was always with."

"Yeah, I know," I said.

"And, of course, once he's with me, then, how? Because he's huge. But, what's more, if there's even a trace of DNA, they can find you, even years later. And then, there are cameras everywhere. Well, almost everywhere. I decided the homecoming game was perfect, because a camera might pick up Joe and it might pick up me, but it's gonna pick up a lot of people. Everyone goes to it, right?"

She beamed at me. And when I didn't say anything, she kept going. "I dressed in a jacket with a hood, and not too much underneath. Of course, I had to convince my mom to let me go, because, like I said, she hates me and won't let me do anything. She thought I just wanted an excuse to get out of the house and go see Matt. And even though she knew that was over, she was really suspicious. She knew it was over because she sneaked a look at my diary and we had another screaming fight because I write shit in my diary, you know? Anyway, she almost didn't let me go. But then, she decided going to a football game was wholesome. Oh, my God, the things she thinks are too stupid."

I was losing my patience. The little kids were almost done playing and the sky was getting dark. My dad was probably wondering where the hell I was. "And then?"

"And then I saw Joe." Maddy smiled. she was finally gonna tell me her story.

CHAPTER ELEVEN

I was nervous as hell as Maddy started saying what happened to Joe. I really wanted to get up and run. But I couldn't. I had to know.

"The game started. Joe was with his friends, so I just waited," She began. "Then it was half-time and he got up to go buy food. He was by himself, for once. I cut in line, and was standing close behind him so no one could see me touch him, you know? He turned around and I unzipped my jacket just enough so that he could see. I was not wearing a shirt or anything. He just stared. Of course, he thought I was thinking that he was gorgeous."

Yeah, I could just see Joe believing that.

Maddy kept going. "I kind of jerked my head so he would get the idea I wanted him to follow me. I pulled up the hood on my jacket and I made sure to stay far enough ahead so it wouldn't look like we were walking together. Finally, when we were across the street from the school and there was no one around, I said, 'Why don't you go get your car and I'll wait here.' He was practically slobbering all over himself when he agreed."

I nodded. I had no problem imagining any of this.

"He pulled up in his car and I got in. By now, Joe was wondering what was going on. He finally asked, 'Do I know you?' I said, 'You know Jimmy O'Keefe. He hired me so you'd leave him alone.' Joe said, 'That freak? No way.' I just knew he'd say that, so guess what I thought of? I had these five one hundred dollar bills that I was saving for when I was going to run away with

Matt. I showed him and said, 'Look. It's paid for. You want to do this?' Joe believed me, just because I showed him all that money. And we drove to this fire road near the lake."

I looked around in shock: it was just about a mile from where we were sitting.

"Don't look over there!" Maddy practically jumped out of her skin. "Of course, it's near here. I needed it to be close enough so I could walk home after."

I nodded again.

She calmed down. "So, he parked and I made sure there was no one else around. That was where Matt and I used to park and there'd never be anyone around, ever. Joe was still kind of wondering what was going on. He was so big, it was not like I could just attack him or anything. I had to, you know?"

Maddy kind of flicked her tongue and I said, "Uh-huh," real quickly so she would stop. I didn't really want to think about her and Joe, if you want to know the truth.

"Then, you know what? I thought, OK, I'll give him a chance. I mean, if he said he'd stop bothering you, you'd still owe me, right? It was up to him, not me. I said, 'So, you gonna leave him alone?' Meaning you. Joe said, 'Hell no.' He started laughing really hard and said, 'The nerd should've bought himself a blow job.' I decided, OK, this is your fault."

I was thinking, right, Maddy would believe what she was going do to Joe was Joe's fault.

"I pulled out a lighter from my pocket and said, 'I need a cigarette'. I reached down and started going through my purse, like I was looking for a pack of cigarettes. But what I really grabbed was this big ice-tea bottle that I filled with gas from my mom's car. That was when I noticed Joe's wallet fell out of his pants during...you know. I picked up his wallet, too.

I opened the car door to get out. He wasn't even watching when I spilled the gas and flicked the lighter. You know what? I was not even scared."

I shrugged. That was all I could do; my mouth was too dry to say anything.

"Anyway, it worked. It totally worked. Joe's whole car caught fire. He was screaming like mad. And then, oh my God, just as he got his door open, the gas tank blew up. I mean, everything, the whole car, was just all on fire. Joe stopped screaming, thank God. I thought, cool, DNA is gone. I started walking home, and guess what? It started raining really hard. All I could think was, very cool. Now, footprints were gone. By the time I heard a fire truck, I was already across the street and far away. No one saw me."

I totally believe she did what she said. It was like she was some kind of criminal genius. Too late. I figured that it would've been better if I didn't know what happened. Now that I knew, it was like I was part of it.

"Now, you owe me," she said. She got up and left me sitting on the grass.

I was scared out of my mind.

CHAPTER TWELVE

It took forever to walk home after talking to Maddy. By now it was dark. All through the walk, I thought about her story and imagined her doing everything she said she did.

I saw her getting out of Joe's car and throwing the lighter at him. I didn't even hate Joe anymore; I just felt completely sorry, like I wished I could apologize to him or something, even though I'd tell him it was not my fault.

It really wasn't my fault. I kept going over the conversation after Joe beat me up and Maddy said, "Do you want it to stop?" I was so out of it. All I thought was, of course, I wanted Joe to stop. I kept asking myself, why didn't I understand what she was saying and put an end to her insane plan right then and there? I thought of all kinds of things I could've said. I had about a hundred conversations in my head where I told Maddy, "No way, are you kidding?" and "Go away! You're crazy!" But I knew I was just driving myself nuts. Nothing could change what had already happened.

When I got home, I expected Dad to be mad at me for returning late. He didn't even see me. He was on the phone. I went to my room, 'cause I was afraid that if I talked to him, he would notice that something was really wrong. I blasted my headphones so loud they hurt me. The idea was: if the music was loud enough, I would be distracted and not think about whether I should tell him about it or not. It actually worked for a while; I couldn't think about anything.

I put the TV on and kept looking over to see if there would be a story about Joe. Finally, I saw a TV announcer. As he talked, there was this headline 'Teen Murder' and a picture of Joe. I tore off my headphones. The announcer, a silver-haired guy, was saying: "...in the bizarre death of a local teen who was last seen at an Oak Ridge High School football game..."

He looked very solemn, like that made what he was saying true. "According to the El Dorado County sheriff's department, the murdered teen had been involved in an ongoing altercation with another boy at the school. Because he is a juvenile, his name has not been made public."

Altercation? I was thinking, this is total bullshit. I was completely disgusted how the TV news got it wrong.

The TV picture switched to a young reporter standing in front of a law office while the announcer said: "In a Channel 0 exclusive, reporter Dave Perez spoke to Hank Larsen, a lawyer for the boy's family."

That was the first I heard anything about a lawyer. I started to run out of the room, but I stopped, because I figured I had better hear what he had to say. Dave Perez was talking to some lawyer who had a mountain of law books all around him: "We understand that your client - and the boy who was murdered- had a long-standing problem."

Mr. Larsen was cool. He looked like a guy about 30-years-old with a beard. He spoke like a professor who could make something sound so incredibly simple, you'd feel like an idiot if you didn't believe him. "My client was three thousand miles away at the time of the murder. Three thousand miles away." Just him saying this made Dave Perez get the expression like he made a really stupid mistake.

But once the TV switched to Dave Perez standing outside the law office again, he was back to being sure of himself. "Off camera, Mr. Larsen noted that there had been a recent uptick in local drug crimes. Could this murder simply be a case of a drug buy gone wrong?" I couldn't help but think how pissed off Joe's dad would be if he was watching the program and heard that.

When I found my dad, he was still on the phone, the same TV news program was still on, and he was thanking someone I figured was Hank Larsen.

I waited until he hung up. "Dad, I don't need a lawyer." "Of course, you do." The way he said it made me cringe.

"You think I had something to do with this?" After I said this, I immediately wished I hadn't. Why give him the chance to even consider that question?

"I think you had nothing to do with this," he said. I was relieved until he added, "But the police will, at some point, want to talk to you. And I don't want something stupid to happen."

I had no idea what he meant by something stupid could happen, but I figured there was no way he could know anything about Maddy. I decided the best thing was to go back to my room and not say anything more. But before I turned to leave, Dad presented another big surprise, a brand new MacBook Pro.

"It might be some time before you get your other one back," he explained.

For a split second, I was blown away. It was cool of my dad to do that. I looked at him and that was all I could do in order not to start crying or something. Right then, I knew I wasn't going to tell him about Maddy. He thought I was all emotional because I was so happy. He gave me this big hug, but it just made me feel worse. I was going crazy. I really was.

CHAPTER THIRTEEN

Of course, the first thing Jake said the next day was, "Drug buy gone wrong? Dude, seriously?"

We were sitting in the cafeteria. I shrugged. "Really, not my problem."

"Well, you know what your problem is?" Jake continued. "The cops have video."

"What video?" I didn't bother asking Jake how he knew this. Jake had tapped into a lot of what was going on at school, 'cause he was always on Facebook, Twitter, and Instagram. He practically had to post a picture or something, like, every five minutes.

"A couple of the coaches were filming. They got shots of the crowd. They figured Joe left with someone he met at the game."

"Do you get I was in New York?"

"Dude, someone's in that video," said Jake. "And that someone wouldn't be me."

"There are all kinds of ways to make things happen," Jake suggested darkly.

"Right," I said, a bit cynical.

But Jake wouldn't let go. "You gotta admit, no one hated Joe as much as you."

That was when I noticed Greg and Zack at another table. They were staring, just staring, at me and Jake. Here jake was trying to get me to say I conspired with someone to kill Joe, and Greg and Zack were thinking, yeah, and that person was Jake. It would be funny if it wasn't so goddamn sick.

After gym, I found out I was right about what Greg and Zack were thinking. Just as I slammed my locker shut, I looked up and saw them standing in my way. I was gonna have to listen.

Greg said, "We've seen you talking to Jake. Kind of funny, you having so much to talk about."

Zack chimed in. "Maybe Jake's in on it."

I couldn't help myself. I had to tell them how stupid they were. "Why would Joe be alone in a car with Jake? Or didn't you get that far?"

Greg suddenly became hostile. Even he saw that the idea was dumb. He set his jaw like he was right, though he knew he had no clue. "Joe was set up. I don't know how, but he was set up."

"Great. Work on the knowing how," I said.

Immediately I said this, I thought to myself, I'm the one who's being stupid. I had practically told them, go figure out who Joe would want to be alone with in a car. Luckily, Greg and Zack didn't look like they got it. I started walking away. Fast. Just as I was leaving the gym, Coach Johnson saw me.

"O'Keefe!" he yelled. "They want you! In the principal's office!

Now!"

Instead of going to my next class, which I actually needed to get to, I had to go to the principal's office. Since I had never been there, I figured it had to be about Joe. I had no idea what Principal Bachman was going to say.

As I was walking to the office, I saw Lila. She was standing by the school's counseling center, trying to hand out flyers, but nobody took one. I kind of felt bad for her. I walked over and was about to grab a flyer when she saw it was me. Instead of giving me the flyer, she said, "You probably don't want this."

That was when I saw what was on the flyer; a big picture of Joe. The picture was from the last Oak Ridge yearbook. In it he was smiling. If you didn't actually know him, you'd probably think Joe was just some normal dude. Looking at his picture kind of freaked me. It took a moment before I saw the words 'Grief Counseling - Last Day Is Today - - p.m.'

"Yeah, I don't think so," I agree.

"How about this one?" Lila asked. She handed me a different flyer that said 'Youth & Government.' Youth & Government is a club where kids are taught how to be world leaders or something. I mean, any dude in high school who thought he wanted to be a politician was probably already an egotistical jerk, and anyone who was only in the club just to have something to put on a college application was just a different kind of jerk. Except Lila wasn't like that. She was probably the one person in the whole school who actually cared about other people and all. Even though I was about as interested in Youth & Government as I was in grief counseling for Joe, I didn't want to be rude. I looked at the flyer like I was actually considering it before handing it back.

Then Lila said, "About the other day..."

"Look," I interrupted. "I know you were just trying to be nice. I'm sorry."

"No, you were right," Lila smiled. "Totally. I mean, it's cool when someone says what they really think, right to your face."

I smiled, too. For about five seconds, I felt good, but I was not sure what to say. That's the thing about nice people, especially nice girls: sometimes you don't know if a nice girl likes you, or if she's just being nice 'cause she's like that to everyone. I remembered I had to get to Principal Bachman's office, so I said, "Yeah, well. I gotta go."

But before I did, Lila said, "Wait. Jimmy. You didn't have anything to do with this, did you?" And, of course, she meant Joe.

I had my excuse down pat. "I was three thousand miles away." "Yeah," said Lila. "It's just so weird, you know?"

"Yeah," I agreed, and walked away before she could say anything more. With someone like Jake, I was a fantastic liar, but lying to Lila was a whole lot harder.

I got to the principal's office. I was thinking I would have to explain to the secretary why I was there. And since I didn't actually know, I was wondering what to say. But the secretary, this older woman, seemed to know who I was. She looked at me, curious, like she was inspecting me.

"Someone wants to see me?" I asked. "Go right in, they're waiting."

They? I wondered. When I opened the door, I saw that, right there, sitting next to the principal, Mr. Bachman, was Deputy Baker. Before I could ask what Deputy Baker was doing there, Mr. Bachman said, "Jimmy. Sit down."

Mr. Bachman was this middle-aged guy. You could tell, he was used to being in control. The way he said stuff, you were just supposed to do it. He sat at this big desk. There was nothing on it except a computer. The big desk was only to show how important he was. I sat down. Mr. Bachman said right away, "We know you were having a problem with that boy who was killed. I want to understand what was going on between the two of you."

I looked over at Deputy Baker who just sat there, not saying anything. "I thought he's not supposed to be asking me questions without a lawyer," I said.

Mr. Bachman was real smooth. "He's not asking you questions; I'm asking you questions. He's observing."

Seriously, I thought, this was bullshit. I'm a kid and I know this is bullshit. "Really," I said. Even though it was Mr. Bachman, I didn't even try to hide what I was thinking.

"Jimmy, the school has a code of conduct, and if you do not meet that code of conduct because you engage in fighting or other prohibited behavior, then the school has no choice but to take disciplinary action."

I couldn't believe what I was hearing. "You're gonna expel me for not talking to you?" I stood up. Mr. Bachman looked totally surprised. I guess he wasn't used to someone standing up before he was done talking. But I was pissed off because he thought I was too stupid to know what he was doing. "Hey, I'm fine with that," I said. "Go ahead and try. But you know what? My dad's gonna go nuts."

My dad would go nuts if I even told him about Mr. Bachman, which I decided, right there, I would not do. I left before he could say anything more. I didn't even look back to see how annoyed he and Deputy Baker probably were. I didn't enjoy any of what happened one bit.

I hoped they would try to expel me. Then I could go somewhere else, to a school that Maddy didn't go to. And on the way out, just to make my life complete, I saw her. She was looking at something posted on the wall. Right away, I knew it was the flyer about Joe. It was kind of creepy, because Maddy had this secret little smile as she looked at it. She didn't see me. Thank God. But as I walked back to my class, I noticed that the flyers where posted all over the whole damn school. I saw Joe's picture again and again as though his eyes were following me everywhere.

That night, I found out Jake was right. There was a video. I was sitting with my dad at dinner and the TV was on. He usually never had the TV on at dinner, because it was the only time I couldn't wear my headphones or think of an excuse to walk away if he said something I didn't want to hear. He usually kept the important stuff to tell me at dinner, just for that reason. It was like the time Mom walked out and I didn't know if she was coming back: I found out at dinner.

The TV news was on was because Dad thought there could be another story about Joe. And there was. This one news program had a list on the screen about the stories coming up next, just in case you were thinking of turning off the TV or changing the channel or something, and the next story up was 'Teen Murder.'

Shortly, Dave Perez was on the TV. He was standing in front of the Oak Ridge football field. Right away, he said, "This is where a local teenage boy spent his last hours before he was murdered in a gruesome homicide." I shuddered at the word 'gruesome.'

He started getting into his story: "The sheriff has released video taken by the school's coach at the game. So far, detectives have said little and it's not clear if they're making much progress in the case. The boy's family is offering a $0,000 reward for

information that leads to the person - or persons – responsible..."
While he was saying all this, the TV showed the video. The
football coach was supposed to be taping game plays, but what
was in the video were shots of the crowd. That was because
what the coach was really doing was taking pictures of cute
girls; you could tell because the camera kind of lingered on
them. It was actually kind of embarrassing.

Then the video freezed. There was Joe. He was standing next
to Greg and Zack. Over his head was this little arrow that had
been added, just so you don't miss him. Then the camera caught
Maddy. Even though it was probably for only a second, it felt
like the camera stayed on her forever. I was totally freaking.
At the same time, I was trying not to let my dad notice I was
freaking. I had to remind myself that there was nothing to
connect her with Joe. Like she said, she was there but so were
a lot of other people.

"Not much progress," Dad agreed unhappily. He wanted them
to figure it out since he was sure it had nothing to do with me.
I just sighed. I couldn't take anymore of it.

But there was more. Dad kind of cleared his throat and I knew
he was about to say something I didn't want to hear. "We're
meeting with Mr. Larsen the day after tomorrow. As soon as
I get back."

"Dad, why?"

"I think it's a good idea," he said and started eating again.
I knew it was useless to say anything else. I hate dinner. I
really do.

CHAPTER FOURTEEN

Jake was watching me. It was lunch and I was in the cafeteria. I went to sit with him like I always did. I didn't see him at first until I noticed him at a table way across the room. He was holding a book close up to his face like he was reading it. I knew it was crap because if Jake wanted to read something, he read it on his laptop. I knew what he was up to; he wanted to see who I talk to when I felt no one was watching. Just when I thought he was my friend, he did something to make me think otherwise.

Later that afternoon, I was at Mr. Larsen's office. I tried not to look at this other dude who was waiting. The dude couldn't be more than three or four years older than I was. He didn't look like a criminal or anything. I figured if I started watching him, he was going to start watching me, and I was done with anyone watching me. It was creepy enough to be in a criminal lawyer's office without having to wonder why anyone else was there.

Mr. Larsen's office was just down the hill from the high school. My dad was supposed to meet me, only he was late. His flight was delayed. I had been sitting in Mr. Larsen's waiting room for about an hour and a half when what I should have been doing was studying for my algebra mid-term. My dad had already texted me about twelve times to wait. I was not even supposed to think about talking to Mr. Larsen without him.

Then this dude's phone rang and he answered. Maybe it was because I payed him no attention that he started talking like I was not even there. "Yeah, I'm here. Still." The dude listens for a while, then practically exploded. "The whole thing is bullshit. I wasn't even the first. I didn't know she was."

By now, I had an idea what he was talking about. I was trying even harder not to look at him.

"Yeah," the dude said. "He's gonna try to get it thrown out. But if he can't, I'm screwed."

I wished he stopped talking because he was making me nervous. But he didn't. "I mean, why did she have to write about me in her goddamn diary? And why did she leave it lying around, so her mom finds it? She says she'll lie she made it all up, but what if she's lying that she'll lie? She lies about everything. It's so fucked up!"

That was when Mr. Larsen opened the door of the waiting room and said, "Matt." I practically fell out of my chair. Matt was the name of Maddy's boyfriend. Maddy wrote stuff in her diary. Maddy's mom found her diary. He was talking about Maddy.

Mr. Larsen immediately noticed that I was looking freaked. But Matt got up, so Mr. Larsen had to pay attention to him instead. They both walked back to Mr. Larsen's office while I sat there trying to put it all together. Maddy's mom turned in Maddy's diary to the police. The two of them hated each other, and now they were gonna hate each other more. That meant, no way was I ever gonna be able to talk Maddy out of anything.

I was thinking of how weird it was that this dude, Matt, would be in the same room with me. Then I realized it wasn't all that strange. El Dorado Hills was really a small place and, mostly, everyone was pretty law-abiding. There probably wasn't a need for a whole lot of criminal attorneys around there.

Finally, my dad walked in. He was still in his pilot's uniform and he looked tired. He hated it when there was even a five- minute delay on one of his flights. This one was three hours! All I wanted to do was tell my dad everything, but I couldn't.

It was like, with that dude, Matt, there, Maddy was there, too. So, I didn't say anything. My dad closed his eyes like he was resting, but I knew it was because he figured that I was anxious as hell and didn't want to talk. At last, the office door opened and Matt walked out.

I couldn't help looking at him when I heard my dad whisper, "Don't stare." I had to stop myself from laughing; it was all too messed up.

Then it was our turn. Mr. Larsen's office had even more books than I saw on TV. There were bookcases that went from the floor to the ceiling on every wall, and every one of them was crammed full. I was looking at all that stuff. When I looked back, I saw Mr. Larsen looking right at me. He didn't even bother pretending he wasn't looking. I kind of flushed and looked down like I had something to hide. I did any way.

Mr. Larsen kept looking straight at me as he started explaining things: "So, at some point, when they know more, the detectives will want to talk with you. And that's not a problem as long as I'm there. But bad things can happen when a kid gets left alone with a cop. Ever heard of the Michael Crowe case?"

I shook my head and so did my dad.

"A-year-old girl was killed by a transient. The cops interrogated her -year-old brother and two of his friends. For hours. They were brought to trial on forced confessions, and the fact that young Michael liked to wear black." I looked down at my tee shirt. Yeah, it was black. So were my jeans. And so was my all-black converse.

"Luckily," Mr. Larsen said, "there was physical evidence that exonerated them."

"Jimmy was with me," my dad said quickly. "He wasn't involved."

"Yes, well, all they need is a theory to ruin people's lives."

If Mr. Larsen was trying to make me feel better, he was doing a lousy job. I smiled. But it was this dumb smile like I didn't even believe in myself.

Mr. Larsen noticed my expression. "You OK?"

I was not OK. Not by a long shot. "Yeah," I lied.

Mr. Larsen frowned. I could tell he knew I was lying. I hated lying. I was thinking he was about to ask me something else, and, if he did, I knew I was going to blurt something out. But all he said was, "We're done for today." He stood up to show it was time for us to leave. My dad and I got up, but Mr. Larsen pulled me aside just after my dad walked out of the office. "Be careful what you say to anyone. Even as a joke."

I nodded. I didn't mind Mr. Larsen saying that. It was probably pretty good advice. But what freaked me was that he didn't want to say it in front of my dad. I didn't want to think about what that meant.

CHAPTER FIFTEEN

I was walking to class when I heard a girl's voice right behind me. "Are you avoiding me?"

I froze, thinking it was Maddy. I knew Maddy wanted to talk to me. I could feel it, even if I hadn't actually seen her for days. So, when I whirled around and saw it was Lila, I practically fell over from sheer relief.

"Oh, hi," I managed.

"Well, are you?" Lila asked. She was smiling, but I could see she was not gonna be satisfied with a bullshit answer. And the fact was, I had been avoiding her because the last time I saw her, she asked if I had anything to do with what happened to Joe, and that was not exactly something I wanted to talk about. Now, I had to lie to her, even though, like I said, I hated lying. "No. I mean, I didn't have your phone number."

"Really," she said. I knew that she didn't totally buy it. But she was not mad or anything, she just had something to tell me. "Jimmy," she began. "You know that counseling stuff about Joe?"

I remembered the flyer with Joe's yearbook picture. I didn't like having to remember Joe's eyes staring at me, but I nodded.

"Well, I went. I'm trying to start a peer counseling program here at Oak Ridge, and I thought, you know, maybe I would learn something."

Lila was always thinking of a way of helping someone. "Yeah?" I said.

"It was a group session. Except that, you're not allowed to talk about what anyone said. You have to swear you won't."

Lila would rather die than break some dumb rule. Then it hit me. For God's sake, who else would be there except Greg and Zack?

"Jimmy, be careful. OK?"

"Lila, did they say what they were going to do? Greg and Zack, I mean?"

Lila looked relieved I got it without her having to tell what anybody said.

"No. They're just ..." She looked at me helplessly, like it would be a crime if she said anything more.

"Insanely pissed off," I said. She nodded, then walked away. Too late, I remembered I forgot to get her phone number. But now, I was left wondering just what the hell Greg and Zack were planning to do to me. It was not a good feeling.

If anyone knew what someone else was up to, it was Jake.

I saw him in the locker room at gym and went right up to him. "What's going on with the creeps?" I asked. I looked at him straight on. I wasn't going to give him a chance to deny he knew something.

"Heh. Heh. Heh." That was the sound Jake makes when he laughs.

"Yeah?" I said.

Jake was nervous, because Greg and Zack could be near. "Tell you at lunch," he said. I thought about it, then nodded OK. Yeah, Jake knew something, all right.

I half expected Jake to try to duck out at lunch, but he didn't. He was even sitting in his same old seat. "Well?" I said.

"They wanted me to set up a web cam. They said they'd cut me in on that 0 K reward."

That's pretty much what I thought. "So, did you?" "Dude, like I'd ever break the law for them," said Jake.

I thought about Jake's answer. He didn't exactly say he didn't do it, just that he didn't do it for them. I doubted if he had done it yet. But I got the idea he was thinking about it.

"What?"

"They're so lame. I was kidding around. So, I said, why don't you just grab Jimmy and torture him if you want to find out what he knows. They thought that was a great idea."

"Thanks," I said, sarcastic. Then I fowned. What if...? "Dude, they're too stupid to figure how to do it." "Maybe not," I said. Maybe they're just smart enough.

I figured that Jake was actually kind of enjoying telling me this. He knew it was going to get me worried. I was about to tell him he was a dick, but I didn't. I still needed Jake to keep me posted about what the creeps were up to. Yeah, I hated my life.

A couple of nights later, I was at home by myself. It was Halloween. There was a bunch of parties I knew about, but I decided not to go to any of them. I didn't want to risk running into Greg and Zack. Not on Halloween. My dad was away, so I figured I should just answer the door and give out candy. The little kids came in these big groups, eight or ten of them, all dressed up. The really young kids cracked me up, 'cause they were totally into it. They were, like, I am Spiderman. I am Superman. So, when the bell rang, even though it was kind of late, I didn't think anything and just opened the door. Only, this time, it was Maddy. She had a big hat and this vampire mask that covered her whole face. I didn't know who it was at first.

"Don't be a jerk," she said. "It's me. Let me in."

I didn't move. I didn't want her anywhere inside my house. "You want to talk at school? With Joe's douche friends watching?"

I hesitated.

"But hey. If you'd rather."

I let her in and quickly closed the door behind her. "You a vampire this year, Maddy?" I said. "You didn't need to bother with a costume."

She laughed and took off her hat and mask. She didn't care what I thought of her, that was for sure. She glanced around. She picked up a picture of my dad and I and looked at it curiously before putting it down. "Your dad here? No, of course not, or you wouldn't have let me in."

I decided it was a really bad idea that I let her come inside. And I hated that she even mentioned my dad. "You got 0 seconds," I told her.

Maddy looked at me like I was an idiot and took off her jacket. She was wearing a costume that was black and tight. I couldn't help noticing how good she looked.

"Your dad isn't home and you want me to go?" Maddy's voice was taunting.

I wanted her to go. But I had to admit, I didn't. She was looking like she'd let me kiss her. Maybe more. For a moment, I was confused as hell. Suddenly, I thought of her boyfriend, Matt.

"And end up like your boyfriend?"

"What do you know about that?" she asked, suspicious.

"Why do you write stuff in a diary? You knew what your mom would do if she found it."

Maddy grinned. She wanted to tell, and I was the only one she could tell. "I wanted Matt to hate my mom as much as I did. So, he'd help me. Only," she shrugged, "he wouldn't."

I understood that she set him up. It was stunning, really.

"But you know what? I don't need him any more." She smiled. "Don't worry, I won't write about you."

I wanted her out immediately.

"Just say what you came to say," I told her.

"The address is 2164 Oak Court. How you do it is up to you."
"You're crazy," I said.

"Listen, O'Keefe..."

"No, you listen. I wasn't there. You were. And there's nothing that ties me to what happened, except you. But you can't turn me in without turning in yourself."

Maddy was ready for me. "Joe had his driver's license with him, on account of, he died in his car. Your fingerprints are all over it, not mine. I can send it to the police. They'd never know who it came from."

"I'd tell them," I said.

"And if you did, I'd swear the whole thing was your dad's idea."

I was sarcastic. "Like they'd believe you?"

"It was your dad who arranged your incredibly good alibi, and your dad who wouldn't let you talk to the police. Everyone would believe me."

She was right. She was goddamn right, I thought. Maddy smiled her cat's smile. She knew she had me.

"You're evil, you know that?" I said slowly. "You're some kind of evil witch."

"That's right, O'Keefe. I'm a witch and I've put a hex on you. And there's just one way to get it off."

"Get the hell out," I said as I opened the front door.

Maddy took care to put on her hat and mask before leaving. "November th," she said. "I changed your life once. I can do it again." She walked out the door and into the dark. I stared after her like I had just seen the Devil. Then I slammed the door as hard as I could.

CHAPTER SIXTEEN

Mr. Larsen was right. The detectives wanted to talk to me. Mr. Larsen told my dad it probably meant the detectives were done digging up things to ask me about. He said it could mean they probably wouldn't bother me for a while. I felt it was crazy to be happy about talking to a detective, but I didn't tell him this. My dad wasn't allowed to be there, only Mr. Larsen.

Mr. Larsen and I were sitting in a little room with Deputy Baker, and, even though I couldn't see a camera, I was sure there was one. Deputy Baker didn't have a list of questions. He didn't have anything written down at all. That was because he intended to stare at me the whole time, without ever having to look away. I was nervous as hell, but I figured, everyone expected a kid to be nervous. Mr. Larsen was not the least bit nervous. All he told me was not to answer any question unless he said it was OK. He had told me that about fifty times.

Deputy Baker tried to throw me off from the start. "You hated him, didn't you?"

Mr. Larsen jumped right in. "You don't have to answer that," he said.

That meant I was not supposed to answer it, so I didn't. Deputy Baker kept going, like Mr. Larsen didn't say anything. "Well, we've heard from a lot of people that you did. You want to help us out here, Jimmy?"

Mr. Larsen gave me this look like I'd be an idiot if I said something.

Deputy Baker cleared his throat. "Whoever did this had a reason to do it. No one just happens to walk around with a bottle of gasoline in their back pocket. You see the problem, don't you?"

I started to say, "I mean..." I was only going to say, "I mean, yeah, I see the problem," but Mr. Larsen held up a hand. I was not supposed to say anything. I could tell that Deputy Baker was starting to get really annoyed.

"The problem is, you had a reason," Deputy Baker continued. "So, if you had something to do with this, you need to say, 'I know I did something wrong and I need to make things right.' Because suppose we find someone helped you and that person talks first? Then you've put yourself in a much worse situation."

"Is there a question in there?" Mr. Larsen asked.

Deputy Baker thought of one. "You understand what I'm saying?"

Mr. Larsen didn't look like he objected, so I finally said, "Yeah. Sure."

"So, you and this boy were getting into fights. Did you want him to stop fighting you?" Deputy Baker softened his voice like he was my long-lost friend or something. "Did you want to make him stop fighting you?"

Mr. Larsen practically had a fit. "Don't answer that!"

Deputy Baker didn't even bother to hide how irritated he was with Mr. Larsen. "What are we doing here? You're not letting him say anything."

Mr. Larsen was just as pissed off. "If you'd like to ask him where he was at the time of the murder, I'll be happy to let him respond."

"We already know that."

"Then he doesn't need to answer any more questions."

Now, Deputy Baker turned to me, like Mr. Larsen wasn't even in the room, which I knew was gonna get Mr. Larsen furious. "Listen to me, Jimmy. Sooner or later, we're gonna find out who killed that boy."

Mr. Larsen stood and motioned for me to get up, too. "Let's go," he said.

Deputy Baker wasn't finished, though. "And if you had anything to do with it, you'll be very sorry you didn't tell me."

The minute we left the room, Mr. Larsen wasn't angry anymore. Not in the slightest. In fact, he looked kind of amused. But because we left early, my dad wasn't there yet to pick me up. Mr. Larsen called him and said he would drive me home. I figured that he didn't want me hanging around the sheriff's office waiting for my dad by myself. Mr. Larsen didn't want me hanging around the sheriff's office without him, even for one second.

On the way home, I was kind of quiet. All I could think about was Deputy Baker telling me how sorry I would be if I didn't tell him the truth. Mr. Larsen looked at me while he was driving and noticed I was not in a very happy mood. That was when he decided to explain what it meant to be a lawyer.

"You know, you're a smart boy," he said. "You should think about law school."

I wasn't exactly thinking about my future career plans at that moment. I was not sure I even had a future. But I nodded to be polite.

"Being a lawyer gives you the chance to help people. Of course, it's a job with a lot of responsibility. A lawyer is an officer of the court, you know."

I didn't ask what that meant, but, yeah, he was gonna tell me.

"If you're an officer of the court, it means you can't lie."

He was waiting for me to say something to be sure I was actually listening. "OK," I said.

"And that's why sometimes a lawyer will say to a client, 'Don't tell me anything,' because, if a lawyer knows a story is false, he can't ethically allow that story to be presented to the court as if it's true."

"I get it, Mr. Larsen. I do." And I truly did. Mr. Larsen didn't want to hear anything I couldn't say to the cops. It was not a great feeling to know Mr. Larsen didn't have a lot of confidence in me at that moment.

That night, I was in my room going crazy. I figured I had three choices and all of them were bad. I could tell Mr. Larsen the truth. But then I couldn't pretend I knew nothing about Joe any more. Plus, Maddy would get me sent to jail if I said anything. I was sure of that.

Or I could do nothing. Except, Maddy would get mad and send the cops Joe's driver's license with my prints, just like she said. She'll figure out a way to let them know it was me, all right.

And I won't get to explain because she'd say, yeah, it was my dad's idea.

Or I could do what Maddy wanted.

It was insane even to have thought about doing what Maddy wanted.

CHAPTER SEVENTEEN

I couldn't talk to anyone.

It was almost a week since I got questioned by Deputy Baker and I had spent every second asking myself the same thing over and over: what the hell am I gonna do? If I could just talk to someone, maybe I wouldn't be as seriously messed up as I was. I felt even wor se than when I was being bullied by Joe. At least, then, I didn't hate myself, I hated him. I kept thinking there had to be a way out of this. But I didn't know what it was. I couldn't talk to my dad; he might persuade me to say the truth, no matter what. But what if he thinks no one will believe me and doesn't want me to tell? If the cops ever figure things out, then he could get in trouble. Maybe even in as much trouble as me.

I couldn't talk to Mr. Larsen because I had to know what I wanted to do before I talked to him. And I definitely couldn't talk to any of my friends. Jake would probably have sold me out to get the reward Joe's parents put up. I mean, I knew he would. 'Cause I get it, $ 0,000 is a whole lot of money. That's why they offered a reward, so someone would sell you out. He wouldn't even feel bad about it, since what happened to Joe was so creepy. And Lila? Even if she swore not to tell, she would. She'd think about it and decide she had to. She wouldn't take a dime and she'd feel terrible. But she'd tell all right.

I had no idea what to do, and the time for deciding kept getting closer and closer. The date Maddy told me was only a week away. That was seven days. At school, I was sleepwalking through my classes. During lunch, I was back to hiding in the library.

I was hiding in the library when I saw Lila. She was sitting at a table. I couldn't see if she was with someone because she was partly hidden by the book stacks. As I was about to leave, she looked up that second and saw me. I felt that she would have more questions if I left without saying anything, so I stepped towards her.

Just as I was about to say, "Hey, Lila…" I saw she was sitting with someone. The person was Maddy. I stood there freaking out. I couldn't say a thing.

I couldn't tell what Lila was thinking, but she just said, "Jimmy, you know Maddy?"

"Uh…no." I could barely get the words out. Then, to make sure there was no doubt about it, I said, "No! I don't."

Maddy couldn't help but smile at how lame I sounded. "Hi, Jimmy," she said, like she had never met me before. She didn't have any trouble lying. She was a great liar.

"Maddy and I are going on the same trip this weekend," Lila said.

"Yeah…?" I was thinking, what? Then it hit me. Maddy was going on the Youth & Government trip with Lila. It was overnight and miles from here. The trip was Maddy's alibi.

"I'm sorry, you wanted to say something?" Lila asked. She looked at me strangely. She could see how weird I was acting, but she didn't know why.

"No. Uh, I mean, you're already busy this weekend," I managed, then I walked away.

Just my luck. On my way out, I ran into Greg and Zack. I could tell they were there for a reason, like, maybe they were watching me. I couldn't imagine any other reason they'd be hanging around the library. For a moment, we were all staring at each other and none of us moved. I had already decided that I wasn't going to let Greg and Zack take Joe's place. So, I went right up to them and said, "You got a problem?"

Zack grabbed Greg's arm, like he had to stop him from punching me. I figured they had to be planning something, or Greg would've punched me right there.

Greg glared at me, "No, but you will."

Future tense. Yeah, I thought as much. They were planning something.

As I walked away, I started thinking about what Greg and Zack would do if I ever ended up telling what happened to Joe. They'd never believe I had nothing to do with it. I knew it. Even if everybody else in the world believed me, they wouldn't.

My dad wasn't home that night, and it made me really nervous to be by myself. I had to calm down, but I didn't know how. Maybe it was because of getting freaked by Greg and Zack, or maybe it was because I hadn't slept too well in days. I was beginning to think that the only thing I could do was what Maddy wanted. That was when I realized that I had never seen Maddy's house. Maybe if I actually saw her house, I would figure out that.

I set the alarm for 5 a.m. I felt it would still be dark, but, if someone saw me, I would say I was in training or something. 2 a.m., you're a criminal; 5 a.m., you're just trying to make the team. By the time it was 5 a.m., I still had not slept. I took my bike and rode down the hill. There were a few cars on the road. I wore a helmet and no one slowed down to see who I was.

Maddy's house wasn't far and it was quite easy to find. I stopped like I was catching my breath or something. Actually, I was. The house was all stucco and there was a fenced yard. I figured I could get over the fence, but I'd have to break a window to get inside. That would wake whoever was there. I was kind of relieved, thinking to myself, "No way can I do this." All of a sudden, this big dog came charging out of the house into the yard and started barking at me. It was a black lab. Black labs might look fierce, but they're not. Then I got it. There was a dog door. Maddy didn't have to tell me; she knew I'd figure it out. Now, I couldn't discourage myself from doing this anymore. I had this sinking feeling, like everything was spinning out of control. It was like, I was not me anymore. It was a weird feeling, like I was outside myself. I might have to do this, I thought. I might have to do this. I couldn't believe what I was thinking. I got back on my bike and started pedaling home, one foot, then the other, like I was a zombie.

The next few days went by in a haze. Then it was Friday morning, the day before. I was in a panic because I still hadn't decided what I was gonna do. I was getting off my bus at Oak Ridge when I saw a bunch of kids getting on this other bus. Everyone was loaded down with sleeping bags and backpacks. I saw Lila. Then I knew it was Maddy's trip. Lila had a clipboard and was checking off everyone's names as they got on.

Suddenly, I had the idea to tell Lila not to let Maddy on the bus. If Maddy didn't go, then it couldn't happen. That was how crazed I was. Like if I could just stop Maddy from getting on the damned bus, everything would be OK.

I was standing there thinking about all this when a car horn blared right behind me. It was some older woman in an SUV and she was really annoyed. "Come on, I haven't got all day."

As I stepped out of the way, I saw Maddy beside her and it hit me: it was Maddy's mom. I stared at the woman, then I stopped. I didn't want to know what she looked like. But it was too late, I had already seen her. Maddy got out of the SUV, and I heard her say, "Actually, Mom, you do have all day." Then Maddy looked at me, amused as hell. "But that's all you have," she said softly, so only I could hear. She walked past me and I just knew, yeah, there was no way I could stop her from getting on that bus.

Somehow, I managed through the rest of the school day. I went home and crashed. I could sleep forever.

My dad got home. I was lying in bed and I didn't move. I didn't want to leave my room. I heard him yell, "Jimmy!" like he was wondering if I was home. I turned up the music way loud so he would know I was around.

He opened the door of my room and stood in the doorway. "Jimmy!"

I nodded but I didn't say anything. This time, he had something he needed to tell me, no matter how loud the music was playing.

"Jimmy! That clip was on TV again."

He meant the video that showed Joe at the football game. "I don't care," I said. And I didn't.

"Same clip," he said. "Maybe they don't have anything new."

"I don't care, Dad," I said again, and I turned up the music even louder. I just couldn't talk to him at that time. He looked at me like he knew something was wrong, but all he said was,

"Keep it down, I've got to…"

I finished his sentence for him. "...get up early." I turned off the music and asked, "You're back when?"

"Sunday night."

"Yeah," I said. If my dad was gonna be here, that might have been enough reason to stop me. But he won't be here. All my excuses were gone. I closed my eyes. I just wanted it all to go away.

CHAPTER EIGHTEEN

I had a plan.

I was at the market near my house trying to remember what I needed. I had to keep everything in my head. No lists. It would be crazy to write a list; that was the kind of thing I could lose or leave lying around. All of a sudden, I cringed. I had started thinking like Maddy. I tried to remember all the stuff I needed for the dog. I made sure to use self-check and pay cash.

There was just one more thing I needed. My dad had this big folding buck knife he used to take when we go camping. I found it jumbled up with some fishing tackle in the garage. The four-inch blade was sharp. I could taste the acid bubbling up from the pit of my stomach as I touched it.

I folded the knife and kept it in my pocket. Somehow, I felt different as I carried it. Then I laid down on my bed and waited. I knew I needed to get some sleep, but I couldn't. I didn't even bother setting an alarm. That was how sure I was that I wasn't going to sleep. Finally, I couldn't stand it anymore. I got up and left the house. The streets were empty as I rode my bike down the hill. I was wearing black, of course. Always, black.

It was a.m. and I was waiting for Maddy's dog to come outside. If it didn't, I would go back. A dog would wake anyone if I tried going inside. At least, I thought it was 5 a.m. I didn't know how long I had been waiting. My bike was behind a hedge, so no one could see it from the street, and I was hiding so no one could see me. I was wearing a beanie and gloves, and was practically shaking. I was so nervous.

Just when I was about to give up, I heard the dog burst through its door. He knew I was there the way dogs knew stuff, and he found me in the yard. He started to growl but I was ready for him. I had a handful of dog treats and I started walking to him slowly.

"Hey, buddy. Sshh, it's all right," I said softly, and I tossed him a treat.

He was a sucker for treats, just like I thought. He stopped barking but started whining for more. "Quiet," I whispered. I gave him another and quickly snapped a leash on his collar. Then I threw a fistful on the ground. As he went after them, I took out a muzzle.

"Sorry, buddy, I need you to be quiet."

I slipped on the muzzle and the dog started going nuts. He hated the muzzle, and now he hated me. He was thrashing around so hard trying to get it off, I could barely tie the leash to a tree. I tried squeezing through the dog door. I couldn't. It was locked. I didn't get it right away; I had seen the dog go inside. Then I saw that it had this tiny electronic device on its collar. I pulled it off and put it in my pocket. It worked; the door opened and I crawled through.

It was dark inside and the tiny flashlight I had was useless. My eyes adjusted to the darkness. I could tell I was in some kind of utility room with a washer and dryer. My shoes were caked with dirt from the yard; I slipped them off so I wouldn't make footprints.

I walked through the house slowly, careful not to make any noise. It was creepy, sneaking around in someone else's house. I thought about leaving. But I told myself that it would be over in a few minutes, so I kept going. I headed up the stairs, pausing after each footstep to listen. But I didn't hear anything.

Then, from one of the bedrooms, I heard the sound of heavy breathing. The door to the room was half closed. I pushed it open inch by inch, and the sound of breathing got louder.

I stepped inside the room. The woman in the bed was lying on her side, and I was glad I didn't have to see her face. I reached out into my pocket and pulled out the knife. For a split second, I felt like I was in absolute control of everything. All I could hear was the beating of my own heart as I started to raise the knife.

Suddenly, I caught my reflection in a mirror opposite the bed. I couldn't believe what I was seeing: me, dressed like a criminal, holding a knife. What the hell was I doing? I stared at the woman and then at myself in the mirror and I gasped. What I was seeing was completely insane. I couldn't move.

Then she turned over and, thinking she was about to wake up, I ran out of the room. I started down the stairs, but I was so panicked, I missed one step and fell, landing in a heap at the bottom. For a moment, I was too stunned to get up. Then I saw the light go on in the bedroom. I jumped up and rushed back to the utility room, grabbed my shoes, and wriggled through the dog door.

The dog was whining and thrashing around as I struggled to put the device back on its collar and slip off the leash. The dog's lunging made it too hard to undo the muzzle, so I cut it with the knife. The second the muzzle was off, the dog bit my hand, and I dropped the knife in the grass. I tried desperately to find it, but it was too dark. I had to step back when the dog started growling. That was when I heard an upstairs window slide open and I freaked. To hell with the knife, I thought. I took off running. The dog followed, barking and growling, as I grabbed my bike and raced down the street.

Maddy's mom must have seen me. But, in the dark, she wouldn't know who I was. At least, that was what I kept telling myself as I rode like a maniac all the way home.

CHAPTER NINETEEN

I never wanted to look in a mirror again. I never wanted to see the person I saw in that woman's bedroom. But I couldn't help it. I kept catching my reflection in the mirror in my room.

And I didn't like what I saw.

The black clothes I wore to break into Maddy's house were in a muddy heap on the floor. I needed to get rid of them. Then I glanced at my closet and noticed I had plenty more just like them. I stared at everything in my room - the black clothes, the death's head tee shirts, the psycho rock band posters, and myself. Just then, I started tearing everything out of my closet and off the walls in a frenzy. I got a roll of big green garbage bags and I crammed all of it, everything, into them. I grabbed scissors and cut my hair as close to my scalp as I could. I didn't stop until it was completely gone. I wanted to be someone else and I didn't care who. Just not me.

Tossing my stuff was the easy part. The hard part was telling Maddy. I had to tell her today, as soon as she was back from her trip, because the sooner I told her, the sooner the person I was will be gone. I slid to the floor and started thinking about how I was gonna do it. I could actually feel how angry she was gonna get. Finally, I had an idea.

It was late afternoon when I got to Maddy's house. I was wearing a red tee shirt and some blue jeans of my dad's. My hair looked butchered, like someone gave me the worst haircut ever, but in a weird way, I kind of liked it. Maddy's mom was in the side yard, so I couldn't try to find the knife I dropped. She didn't see me, and as I got closer, I saw that she was nailing strips of wood across the dog door. The dog wasn't outside, which was lucky; he would have gone nuts if he saw me. I went up the walk and rang the doorbell.

Maddy answered the door. She was furious. "Did you come to tell me you screwed up? I already figured that out! Go away!"

"Not why I'm here," I told her.

"Lucky for you, she thinks it was Matt. And lucky for him, she got scared good and changed her mind about going after him. Only, you know what? Nothing changes between us. Nothing."

"Listen to me."

But Maddy was not listening. "And don't think I'll help you break in, O'Keefe. It can't look like I'm any part of it."

She was trying to shut the door, but I wedged my foot to hold it open. From inside, I heard the dog barking. "Listen!" I said. "Not. Gonna. Happen. Ever."

"What?"

I didn't bother answering and just walked away. I knew it was gonna drive Maddy crazy that I didn't answer her.

When I reached the street, I turned back and saw that I was right, Maddy was still at the door like she couldn't believe what I told her. Then I saw her mom standing near the front of the house, staring at me. I couldn't help wondering if Maddy's mom heard any part of what she and I said. It didn't give me a great feeling, but I had to put it out of my mind. At that moment, I was more worried about Maddy.

I kept walking until I saw a place to hide beside a big SUV parked in front of one of the nearby houses. There was a set of mailboxes just steps from where I was. I didn't have to wait long before I heard someone running along the sidewalk. It was Maddy. I let her run past, then I caught up with her and, from behind, grabbed the envelope she was holding out of her hand.

Maddy whirled around. "NOOOOO!!" she screamed.

"I figured that's what you'd do," I said. "I just had to get you mad enough."

Maddy stared in shocked disbelief that I had outsmarted her. "You asshole!"

"You thought you could bully me to do what you wanted. But no one's ever gonna bully me again."

"We had a deal!"

"We never had a deal!" I insisted. "I didn't know what you were gonna do."

"You think I'm just gonna go away? Really?" "Unless you're stupid - yeah," I told her.

Maddy glared at me. She was pissed as hell. I knew if she could kill me that second, she would. "I'm not stupid. But you are," she said. And she started walking back to her house.

I looked down and saw that the envelope was addressed to the El Dorado County sheriff. Yeah, she was gonna stick it in the mailbox right then. I opened the envelope. Inside was Joe's driver's license, doubled-bagged in plastic. And a typed note. I didn't have to read it. I knew what it said.

I should feel great but I didn't. I knew Maddy meant it when she said she was not going away. As I headed up the hill, I felt uneasy, like something weird could happen any moment.

There was a mini-mall on the corner, and I stopped at a store to get something to drink. I needed to get rid of all the acid I was tasting. I was standing outside drinking a Coke, when suddenly someone in the gym next door knocked on the plate glass window. I was startled and practically dropped the Coke before I saw it was Lila. She was staring at me all shocked. Then I remembered how I looked. I didn't want to talk about it, but she came running outside.

"Your hair," Lila said. "You're different." "Trying to be."

"Why?"

I shrugged, but Lila knew there was something wrong. Something really wrong. "Jimmy. Are you all right?"

I couldn't help but smile. I was definitely not all right, but I didn't want to say something sarcastic.

She just kept staring at me. She looked so concerned that finally I said, "Y'know, you're nice, Lila. Really nice. I wish I'd met you before."

"Before? Before what?"

I was immediately sorry I said anything. "Nothing."

But Lila wasn't stupid. "It has to do with Joe, doesn't it?" Lila said, stunned. "You know what happened."

I could deny it; I could remind her I was thousands of miles away. But I didn't. Because even if I didn't plan it, I knew what happened. And I just couldn't lie about it anymore.

Lila took my silence for a yes. "If you know and do nothing," she began slowly, "you're just like the people who did nothing when Joe went after you."

"Don't you think I get that?!" I exploded.

Lila didn't say anything, but I got the feeling she didn't like me too much now. I couldn't blame her, though, and I didn't try to change her mind. Instead, I turned around and started walking.

By the time I got home, it was dark. I was sitting in my room holding Joe's driver's license and a cigarette lighter. I had already burnt Maddy's note, which I finally did read. If you were a cop and you read Maddy's note, you'd want to arrest me, for sure. I flicked the lighter. I was about to burn Joe's license, then I stopped. I didn't know what to do. If I ever wanted to tell someone what happened, I'd need proof. I mean, without proof, anyone would think I was making it up, it's that crazy.

But then I thought, why would I want to tell someone? It would be suicide to tell someone. Except that Maddy wasn't kidding when she said she was not going away. She was not gonna stop. And if I knew and did nothing, then I was just as bad, like Lila said. I couldn't get Lila's words out of my head.

I looked around my room and saw everything all torn down and crammed in garbage bags. I thought, just throwing away shit was not enough. I either meant it or I didn't.

I was trying to decide what to do when I heard the front door opened.

"I'm home," my dad yelled.

I still wasn't sure what to do. I heard him coming up the stairs. I picked up the lighter and flicked it again so it was flaming. Joe's eyes in his driver's license picture stared at me. Then I flicked the lighter off. I knew.

My dad opened the door of my room and was saying, "Jimmy, I'm..."

But he didn't finish his sentence 'cause he was staring at my butchered hair and my destroyed room.

"Dad, I've got to talk to you."

He was too shocked to say anything. "Dad. Now!"

CHAPTER TWENTY

I was in the kitchen with my dad and I told him everything. The whole time I was talking, he didn't say anything. He just sat there holding Joe's license like he was studying it.

Finally, when I finished, he said, "Why should you go to the police? You didn't do anything."

"Then it can't hurt me, right?" I said. "I don't know. You can't be sure."

My dad was used to being careful. He was used to going through his preflight checklist and shutting down his entire flight if just one thing wasn't perfect. So, he was not exactly leaping all over himself to call Mr. Larsen this second, even if I told him he had to. He needed to think about it first.

"Dad, a boy is dead!" I was desperate for him to call Mr. Larsen. I was gonna lose my nerve if he didn't.

"You can't change that," he said.

I knew what was stopping him. "You don't think I can handle myself, do you?"

"All I'm saying is, don't rush into this."

The way he said it, the answer to my question was probably no. I tried one more time to convince him. "She's not gonna stop," I said darkly.

My dad shrugged. He used to be in the Navy. He flew jets on a warship and was not scared of some -year-old girl, for God's sake, even if I thought he should be. No, he was gonna have to think about it, and think about it some more, before he did anything.

"It's late, Jimmy," my dad said, and he got up to go to bed.

I was way too nervous to sleep, so I made myself a big sandwich and turned on the TV. It was 0 o'clock and the news started. I turned off the sound, but kept the picture on, just in case there was something about Joe. I was eating the sandwich when I looked up at the TV and I practically choked. What was on the TV was Maddy's house. I was sure of it. There was a swarm of cop cars all around and the news guy, Dave Perez, was standing right in front.

By the time I managed to turn up the sound, Dave Perez was saying "...the female victim was found by her daughter just about an hour ago in this house in El Dorado Hills."

"WHAT?!" I screamed at the TV. My dad must have been in the shower because if he wasn't, he would have come running. I was that loud. But I didn't even have time to think about how insane everything was because the next thing Dave Perez said was, "She had been stabbed to death with a hunting knife."

I freaked. It could be the knife I dropped. I was too blown away to do anything except stare at the TV.

"And in a bizarre twist, the victim was able to shoot her attacker just before she died. He, too, is dead."

"Shit!" I gasped.

"The daughter, whose name is being withheld because of her age, is in seclusion at a neighbor's home until family can be reached. But she has confirmed the knife belonged to the young man who committed this brutal attack."

Then the TV showed Mr. Larsen walking up to the house. He looked grim. Though Dave Perez went nuts trying to catch up to him with a microphone, Mr. Larsen ignored him like he didn't even exist.

It hit me. The guy - the attacker - was someone Mr. Larsen was defending, and that could only be Maddy's boyfriend, Matt. But Maddy said her mom was gonna drop charges. So, why?

Unless Maddy was lying. My dad's knife, the one I dropped, was a four-inch folding buck knife with a green camo plastic handle. I knew what it looked like exactly because I stared at it for hours. And if it was mine but Maddy said Matt brought it with him, then she was lying. And if she was lying, there was no way the rest of it happened like they were saying, because no one hated Maddy's mom as much as Maddy.

I was totally freaked. I needed to know if Maddy was lying. I figured if I got to Maddy's house in the next ten minutes, Mr. Larsen would still be there and I could get him to find out about the knife. I had to get there. And I had to get there immediately. You see, the truth was, if the knife was mine and Maddy was lying? I'd be the only other person in the world who'd know it. And she'd know I'd be a danger to her.

I ran upstairs and I heard my dad still in the shower. By the time he'd be out and dressed, even if I could somehow convince him to drive me, it would be too late. I saw the keys to my dad's SUV on his dresser. It took me only about five seconds to decide to grab them and drive myself.

Dad never let me drive his SUV - I didn't have my license yet - but I drove to Maddy's house with no problem. I parked down the street since there was a ton of El Dorado County sheriff's deputy cars, all with their blue and red lights flashing; four TV news trucks, one for each of the local stations; two ambulances; and a bunch of neighbors all piled around Maddy's house. I didn't see Maddy, which was a good thing. But I did see Deputy Baker. I stayed near the news trucks so he wouldn't see me. Finally, I saw Mr. Larsen, who looked even worse than he did on TV.

"Mr. Larsen," I called out, trying to get his attention.

He was shocked to see me. "Jimmy? What are you doing here?"

"I gotta talk to you."

"Go home. This doesn't concern you," he said. His voice was all harsh. He was really upset.

"I think I know who did this."

"So do I. My client killed his accuser. Stupid. Stupid."

I guessed he felt bad for being so hard on me. He was a little nicer when he said, "Jimmy, go home before the deputies see you."

I was about to explain why I was there when a car pulled up and this woman came out. She was shaking like she was so messed up. Mr. Larsen grimaced. "Christ. That must be his mother," he said, and he started walking toward her.

I kept up with him as he walked. "If it wasn't him, I'm in danger. Maybe even my dad's in danger. I need you to go to the cops with me now."

Mr. Larsen put his hand on my shoulder. Yeah, I could tell he wanted me to leave him alone. He probably thought I was crazy. "Not now, Jimmy," he said.

I walked back to where I left my dad's SUV. I was getting in when I looked up at this other house and that was when I saw someone in a second-floor window looking down and watching my every move. There was a light on and I could see perfectly the person watching me was Maddy.

CHAPTER TWENTY-ONE

That was when everything started going completely insane. If only Maddy didn't see me. If only my dad saw me. If only Greg and Zack didn't decide that was the night they were gonna carry out their incredibly stupid, screwed-up plan.

I was driving home from Maddy's, all worried that she figured why I was there. My cell phone rang and I saw it was Dad. If he was calling me, he knew I was not home. I was just hoping that he didn't know his SUV was gone. No such luck. I answered and said, "Dad, I can explain..." But he didn't want an explanation. His voice was pure fury. "You took my car?! You don't even have a license!"

"I had to get somewhere! I'm on my way home!" "You're driving? Get off the phone!" and he hung up.

I couldn't tell him what happened and why I was totally freaked out. I was completely pissed and threw the phone on the seat, and, of course, it fell underneath. I couldn't reach it while I was driving, and I couldn't call him back. Because all this was going on in my head, I was not really paying attention when I saw a car parked out in front of my house.

I pulled up in the driveway and my headlights caught Zack looking in the front window. He whirled around, and I was thinking, what the hell, as I turned off the engine and jumped out after him. He started running back to the street. I was trying to head him off, when I got body slammed from behind by Greg. He fell so he was practically lying on top of me.

"Got him!" Greg said. He was happy.

"Are you freakin' out of your mind?!" I screamed at him.

But Zack was worried. "Dude, I'm telling you, what if someone's in the house?"

I got that they thought my dad wasn't home 'cause his SUV was gone. I was thinking, OK, this is weird, but they're gonna stop. Or they were going to drag me inside and my dad would be there and kick their ass. Fortunately, my dad picked that exact moment to open the front door. Greg and Zack freaked, and Greg held his hand over my mouth to stop me from yelling.

We were on the sidewalk by Greg's car. There was this low hedge in front of my house, and Dad would only have to walk a few feet to see Greg and Zack holding me down. From the ground, I could hear his footsteps as he walked up to his SUV, then I heard him walk straight back to the house and slam the door. I knew he was thinking I cut out to give him time to cool down. He was too angry to take a second to look around.

"Dude, we can't do it here," said Zack.

Greg snorted. "That's not a reason not to do it. That's a reason to do it somewhere else."

Zack said, "Yeah?" like he was not sure, but Greg yanked me to my feet. "You're coming with us."

"Like hell." By now, I remembered Jake joking about telling them to torture me. I struggled to shake Greg off and managed to break free. I took about ten steps to my house when they both grabbed me and Greg came crashing down on me again. I would have yelled for help, but he was covering my mouth even tighter this time.

I noticed that someone hid a security camera in the bushes of my house. I had no idea why it was there. It was not the kind of thing my dad would ever do. I looked to see where it was aimed, maybe the front door and the driveway. But I didn't have time to think about it. The two of them pulled me up and wrestled me into the backseat of Greg's Camaro.

They had duct tape and Greg used it to tape my mouth and hands. He enjoyed doing it. I was like, beyond pissed off. Zack was beside me in the back seat and there was nothing I could do except watch as Greg started his car. Then I saw the headlights of this other car approaching. All of a sudden, it was slowing down. I hoped it was because the driver saw what was going on, even if I didn't know how that could be. Then the other car stopped right by Greg's Camaro. I saw the driver staring inside. I was stunned. It was Maddy and she saw me.

Greg freaked. He had no idea who Maddy was and he didn't get why anyone was stopping to look, so he hit the gas hard and the Camaro lurched forward. I just had enough time to look back and I saw Maddy turning around in the driveway of my house as Greg sped away. She practically hit my dad's SUV. I knew no one could let her use the car she was driving since she was under age. She was such a bad driver. And with Greg speeding like a maniac, I knew he would lose her.

At that moment, I wasn't not even thinking about Maddy. That was because I was going crazy wondering where Greg and Zack were taking me and what they were going to do when they get there. It felt like forever - but it was probably just minutes - before Greg screeched to a stop in front of this house with a 'For Sale' sign and no lights. I was fighting as hard as I could while they were pulling me out of the car. But it was no use. My hands were taped and there was two of them. Greg kicked out a glass panel in the front door and reached through to unlock it. Then they pushed me inside and dragged me to the garage.

Suddenly, I remembered I had been there before. Years ago, when I was a kid. The house was half-empty, like whoever lived there moved out all of a sudden and didn't have time to take everything. Just as I figured where the hell I was, Greg ripped the tape off my mouth. Like he expected me to talk. "This was Joe's house," he said.

"You're gonna tell us what happened to him," said Zack.

Greg felt that was a signal to begin, so he hauled off and punched me in the stomach. I nearly doubled over. But while I was gasping for breath, I used the time to think.

"And what would you do if you found out?" I asked.

"We'd kill the dude," Greg said.

"Right," I said, sarcastic. But the thing was? I knew he meant it.

CHAPTER TWENTY-TWO

Greg was trying to get me to talk, and it was creepy. I'd be an idiot if I told them anything. But Greg was even more nuts than I thought, and Zack was a complete wimp, so there was no one to stop Greg from totally losing it.

We were in the garage of Joe's old house. I was in a chair and my ankles were duct taped to the chair legs. That was Zack's idea. He must've seen it in a movie. Greg found some lighter fluid for a barbecue and he poured some on the floor around me. He lit it, but it burned out immediately 'cause the floor of the garage was cement. Yeah, it was weird, but it looked worse than it really sounded.

Greg thought about it, and, this time, he put crumpled-up newspaper around me and started soaking the newspaper with the lighter fluid. Everything in the garage was packed in boxes so there was plenty of crumpled-up newspaper.

"Are you insane?" I said. I was starting to get nervous that he was gonna figure out what he was doing.

"What happened to Joe?" Greg asked. He lighted a cigarette with his lighter and took a drag. Like he was cool or something, which he was totally not.

"I already told you, I wasn't there."

My answer got him even madder. He took the cigarette and tossed it. The paper went ablaze and burned hot for several seconds. Greg grinned, but Zack looked shocked.

"You dudes are fucking psycho, y'know that?!" I screamed at him.

But all my yelling made Greg feel pleased with himself. "Tell us what happened." I shook my head like I had nothing to say, and Greg started building another ring of newspaper around me. This time he was piling it up closer. Zack watched nervously as Greg squirted the paper with lighter fluid. "Dude, go easy with that," Zack said.

Greg shrugged. "It's what he did to Joe."

Zack's cell phone started ringing but he ignored it. He turned to me and his voice was pleading. "Just tell us what you know, dude!"

I was starting to get anxious as hell. "Like you'd ever believe me," I said.

"See? He does know something!" Greg said.

Greg was convinced he needed to keep on doing what he was doing. And I kicked myself for saying anything.

Greg lighted another cigarette. Zack's phone started ringing again. The sound made him jump. He was so twitchy, but he didn't answer.

"So, dude," Greg said to me, holding up the cigarette. "You wanna smoke?" He held the cigarette so it hovered over the newspapers on the floor around me. "You wanna smoke, get it?"

I didn't answer. I pretty much made up my mind I wasn't going to say one more thing. Zack looked at Greg helplessly.

"Dude," began Zack, when his phone rang again. He answered and screamed into it, "Whoever you are, stop calling me!" He was about to click off when he stopped. "Jake?" As he listened, he looked even more nervous. "I don't know what you're talking about," he said, then jammed the phone back in his pocket.

He turned to Greg all freaked. "That was Jake. He said Jimmy's dad's calling around, looking for him. Jake thinks he's about to call the cops."

"So?" Greg sneered.

"I think Jake knows it's us." "So?"

Zack took in the whole scene: the lighter fluid-soaked paper, Greg and his cigarettes, and me, duct taped to a chair. He looked like he finally got that what they were doing was criminal. "Dude, I'm outta here."

Greg stared at Zack furiously. He grabbed Zack and sent him flying. Zack landed on the cement floor hard.

"We're staying 'til he talks!" Greg screamed. Because he was so pissed, he took the lighted cigarette from where it fell harmlessly, and tossed it right at me. The paper piled up around me erupted. The flames caught the bottom of my jeans and almost fried my converse. I stared at both of them. I couldn't think of any good way this was gonna end.

Greg saw that he had used up all the lighter fluid, and he tossed his lighter on the floor. He started going through the packed boxes, looking for something else he could use to inflict pain. Zack was on the floor, watching, like he was too paralyzed to do anything. Then, all of a sudden, Greg frowned and said, "You smell something?"

I didn't. I realised it was because I had practically stopped breathing. I had to remember to take a breath. When I did, I smelt something, like gas from the stove when a burner isn't turned off properly. Zack didn't care what anything smelt like. "Dude, let's get out of here now."

"Wait," Greg said. He walked off into the house like he was gonna find out. The moment Greg left, Zack got up and started unwinding the tape from my hands.

"I'm not getting screwed 'cause of you," Zack said.

I didn't answer. I didn't want to say anything that was gonna make him change his mind. That was when I heard the sound of a thud from the other room. Zack stopped what he was doing and said, "You hear that?"

"No! Hurry up!"

Zack hesitated, then went back to unwinding the tape. He finished untying my hands, then started working to free one of my feet while I worked on the other. I was frantic to finish before Greg got back, only it was not that easy because the tape was all melted together from the heat. I decided I didn't care how much it hurt. I started ripping it off as hard as I could. It took off skin, but at last my left foot was free. I tried to see how far Zack had gotten, but I couldn't tell. He was bent over my right foot. That was when I saw this shadow looming over us. I jerked my head up, expecting to see Greg.

But it was not him.

It was Maddy. She was holding a baseball bat like she was about to swing it.

For a moment, I was too stunned to do anything. Then I yelled, "LOOK OUT!"

Zack had just a split second to see the bat coming at him. He jerked his body out of the way. The bat missed his head but caught his shoulder with a loud crack. He fell forward, hitting his head on the cement floor. He stayed on the ground, his eyes closed, unmoving.

Maddy started to raise the bat again.

"Leave him alone!" I screamed. "He doesn't know anything!"
"But you do! And I'm not gonna let you tell anyone!"

I was desperately trying to wriggle my foot free, but it was stuck. "Does it look like I told anyone?"

"You were there, at my house tonight, talking," Maddy said.

"Yeah, but you don't know what I said, do you?" I said, and I started to laugh. Like I hoped, it freaked her out. She stared at me uncertainly.

"Want to know?" I said. I had to keep her talking. If I could somehow get my right foot free, I would have a chance. If I couldn't, I had no chance and Zack had no chance as well. I didn't even want to think about why she wasn't worried about Greg.

Maddy hestitated.

"I'll tell you," I offered. "But first, you gotta tell me: what happened tonight?"

Maddy would love to tell, I knew it. She threw a nervous glance toward the door leading from the garage to the house. Suddenly,

I got it. She had turned on the gas. In a few minutes, she was gonna set it off, so the whole house would blow. With me and anyone else - but not her - inside.

Maddy smiled. She had just enough time to tell me how clever she had been.

CHAPTER TWENTY-THREE

"It was your fault," Maddy began. "My mom found your knife. Oh, my God, I couldn't believe you actually left it. And she got scared. She knew someone actually broke in. She thought it was Matt, and I was like, 'OK, just keep thinking that, Mom.' Only, she was not sure."

I was too terrified to say a thing. 'Cause, then, Maddy might stop talking. I just nodded, and she kept going.

"She called Matt and got him to agree to come over by saying she was gonna drop charges. Of course, I didn't believe it. I knew she just wanted to look him in the eye when she asked if it was him. She had this gun because she was paranoid. She pulled it out of her safe, because, now, she was scared of Matt, you know? And I was laughing. She was so stupid. But, then, you showed up and she heard us say stuff, and she knew it was not Matt, it was you. Now, she wanted me to tell who you are, and we got in a big fight, because, duh, I refused. Then she screamed at me, she was going to call the police. I couldn't let her do that. We were fighting and there was your knife, and it just happened."

Maddy took a breath. I had been trying to wriggle my foot out of the tape when she was not looking. I was scared she'd notice, so it was hard to do.

"Then what?" I said quickly. I didn't want her to stop talking for anything. "What about Matt?"

"Oh, him," she said and then giggled. Since I knew he was dead, it was creepy. "I was wondering, what I would do. I was actually thinking of blaming you, when Matt showed up on account of, my mom called him, like I said. And the thing was? I used to like Matt, but now he was nasty to me. He won't even talk to me, he only wanted to talk to my mom. So, I said, 'OK, Matt. You wanna talk to her? Go right ahead, she's upstairs in her room.' When he was upstairs, he bent over her, then looked up and freaked. I asked him to help me, and he said no. There was no way he was gonna help me, and he called me a bunch of shitty names. So, I grabbed my mom's gun. I was thinking, you know it would work; it would totally work, 'cause people would believe he was mad at her. And it really was his fault, you know, for not helping me. Anyway, I had to."

I nodded. I was starting to panic. I couldn't free my foot with Maddy standing there.

"So, I got Matt's fingerprints all over the knife. Then, after, I took another shot with my mom holding the gun, so she got all that stuff on her hands. I jumped in the shower, because my story is, I didn't hear anything, seeing I was in the shower. Then I called the cops, all upset."

Maddy grinned. She was thrilled by what she had done. "And now," she said, "it's your turn."

That was when she saw Greg's lighter on the floor and picked it up. She was gonna run out of there in about two minutes and blast the entire place when she leaves. The smell of gas was overpowering.

I had to do something fast.

"I didn't say anything," I told her. "I kind of knew that if something happened to your mom, it was because of you. But I never said anything. Why would I?"

It sounded totally lame. And as she listened, she got furious. "You're lying. I know you're lying."

Maddy raised the bat and I jumped up. It freaked her that I was standing. But one of my ankles was still tied to the chair, so about all I could do was stop her from hitting Zack. Then she changed her mind and just decided to run out. The moment she did, I frantically ripped off the rest of the tape in seconds and was free. I started racing after her when I slipped on the ashes Greg left all over the floor. I fell hard, but I was very happy I did, because just then the whole house exploded and a shock wave that could've taken me out passed over me instead.

I rolled forward and saw the inferno. The roar of the flames was scary. I only had a few seconds to get out. Then I saw Zack. The easiest way out was climbing through a shattered window, but there was no way I could lift Zack that high. The garage door got smashed by the blast. I tried pulling it open but the frame was bent and I had only a few inches clearance. If Zack got stuck, it was over. I looked at him and hesitated. Then I thought, screw it, I'm not going without him. I grabbed Zack and pushed him head first out the inches-high space beneath the garage door. His shoulders wedged, but I kept pushing. I could barely breathe from the smoke. I felt like I was about to pass out. It was so hot, and I was terrified my clothes were going to catch fire any second.

I kept pushing Zack through until he was out. Then I crawled through myself, dragging him from the house. We were just yards away, when suddenly there was another explosion. I practically lost it when I saw that the garage where we were some moments ago was filled with flames. I grabbed Zack's phone to call for help, but shoved it in my pocket when I heard sirens.

Neighbors started pouring out of their houses. A few of them grabbed garden hoses but, majority of them were just staring. There was no sign of Maddy. I remembered Greg. I looked at the burning house and knew he was still in there.

Zack was finally returning to consciousness. I didn't know what he heard or what he remembered. I was about to find out.

CHAPTER TWENTY-FOUR

I was waving my arms as fire trucks, sheriff's deputy cars and ambulances rolled in. It was a crazy mess of cars and trucks and people running around. "Need some help over here!" I tried yelling. But my voice was choked up from smoke, so it was basically a whisper.

Zack was still on the ground. He looked all dazed. "What... happened?"

I didn't answer. I didn't want to be the one to tell him.

A sheriff's deputy finally saw us and started walking over. The name tag on his uniform was Snyder. I was sure I had never seen him before, but he knew who I was. "Jimmy O'Keefe. You're supposed to be missing."

Missing? So, my dad must have called the police. I only had a moment to think about that when the deputy looked around and realized where he was. "This is that boy's house, the one who died."

Zack was grimacing with pain but he nodded. Deputy Snyder started looking over Zack to see how badly he was hurt. "What were you boys doing?"

Zack struggled to remember. "Trying to find out what happened to Joe." Then he looked at me. "Hey, someone needed to ask him some questions!"

Because Zack was hurt, Deputy Snyder thought Zack was the victim. "You got in a fight? He hit you?"

"No!" I said quickly, but the deputy wanted to hear from Zack, not me.

Zack was totally bewildered. "I don't know," he began. And he didn't know. But then he said, "I mean, yeah. Jimmy musta been freakin' mad at us."

I couldn't believe it. "Dude! No way! I got you out!"

"One at a time!" Deputy Snyder said. "You! Over there! MOVE!"

He meant me, and I had no choice but to go to where he was pointing, a few yards away. As I was walking, I heard Deputy Snyder say, "Us? Who's 'us'?"

I saw Zack staring at Joe's burning house then looking around in confusion. I really didn't want to watch him figure out Greg was missing, and I turned away. I remembered I had Zack's phone, so I pulled it out to call my dad. I figured if my dad called the cops, he had to be pretty worried about me. Too bad, Zack's phone was locked, so I couldn't. That was when I saw Lila. She most probably lived around there, because she was in pajamas like she was asleep or something. I noticed she was holding her cell phone and I walked over to her.

"Lila! Let me use your phone."

She looked shocked when she saw me. "Jimmy! What did you do?"

"Nothing!" I said. She just kept looking at me like I was not saying the truth - not all of it, anyway - but she handed me her phone. I was calling Dad when I heard Deputy Snyder yelling at Zack, "Who else was in that house?!"

I couldn't help it. I looked back to see Zack as he stared from the burning house to Greg's Camaro and his expression became horrified. Then Dad was on the phone. All I wanted to tell him was that I was alive before he saw Joe's burned-out house on TV. But Dad had something to tell me. To get the cops to start looking for me right away, he had to explain I was in danger. Because that was what I told Mr. Larsen, I was in danger.

"Wait? What?"

"Mr. Larsen called the house looking for you," my dad explained. "He was concerned."

I was watching Deputy Snyder trying to calm Zack, who was now completely freaking out. Talking to Mr. Larsen seemed like a million years ago. Only, now it dawned on me. My dad had to tell the police everything I told him.

And that was when he said, "So, the police finally went to talk to her. That girl. Maddy."

"Wait! Dad! When? When did they they go talk to her?" "Deputy Baker left a few minutes ago," he said.

I was frantic as I tried to think how long it had been since Maddy left. I was guessing at least 72 minutes. I could imagine her parking the car she took; it probably belonged to the neighbors where she was staying. She'd park it awfully, but no one would remember how a car was parked in all the confusion, and she'd shoot back into bed at her neighbor's house. If she was fast enough, and lucky enough, and my heart sank because I knew she was, that was where the cops would find her. And that meant, the cops were her alibi. She had the perfect alibi and my dad gave it to her. I couldn't stand thinking about it.

The whole time I was talking to my dad, Deputy Snyder was looking from Zack to me, and his expression wasn't pretty.

"Dad, I...gotta go," was all I could say. I switched off and stuffed the phone back in my pocket.

"I didn't do this, and no one is gonna believe me!" I told Lila. "They're gonna believe her!"

Lila was baffled. "Her?"

I couldn't talk, I was too messed up.

"Jimmy, what on earth are you talking about?"

Finally, I said, "They're gonna say I killed Greg and set the fire to cover it up."

"What?" Lila looked at me like I was insane.

I didn't answer, because just then Deputy Snyder walked up to me when he was done with Zack. There were paramedics with Zack, who looked as though he was in hysterics.

"All right," Deputy Snyder said to me. "It's your turn. Let's hear it."

I look from him to Lila. "OK," I nodded. "OK." At last I said, "You know the girl whose mom was killed tonight?"

Deputy Snyder screamed at me, "I'M IN NO MOOD FOR BULLSHIT!"

I took a deep breath. "Just...let me explain."

I started by telling Deputy Snyder about how Greg and Zack grabbed me, and he nodded. I guess he'd already heard that part from Zack. He got that I didn't go along willingly, but he looked like that only proved what Zack said; how I had to be pretty mad at them. When I started talking about Maddy, I knew I was losing him. He started asking me these dumb questions, like, did I see her hit Greg, and, if I didn't see it, how could a girl overpower a guy? I tried to explain she had a baseball bat, for God's sake, but he just kept saying, "Uh-huh, uh-huh," like he was done listening. 'Cause he didn't believe me at all.

Deputy Snyder didn't seem to care that Lila was hearing all this. She was looking unhappy, like she wanted to believe me, but even she couldn't. Finally, Deputy Snyder felt he had heard enough, and he left to go talk to Dave Perez, the news guy, who had just gotten there.

I turned to Lila. "He didn't believe me," I said. "You don't either, do you?"

Lila didn't say anything. I understood that she didn't want to tell me what she really thought. Finally, she said, "I don't know. Jimmy, I've got to go home."

The atmosphere had started getting bright and the TV crew was setting up for the early morning news. Just then, another sheriff's deputy car rolled up. It was Deputy Baker. He went right over to talk to Deputy Snyder, and I didn't have to hear it to know what they were saying. I was practically beside myself.

"They're gonna arrest me," I told Lila. "They think they've got it all figured out. I just hope they do it before my dad gets here. I don't want him to see it."

"I don't want to see it, either," Lila said. "Jimmy? My phone?"

I pulled a phone out of my pocket and handed it to her. I couldn't take my eyes off Deputy Baker. He was looking satisfied because he thought he had just solved his big ass case. A house was burned up with a kid inside, and he was looking all satisfied.

"This isn't mine," I heard Lila saying, but I was not paying her any attention as she handed the phone back to me. Then I hit the 'on' button and saw it was Zack's. I was about to shove it back in my pocket, when I saw several missed call alerts on the lock screen.

"That's weird," I said when I recognized the number. "All these calls are from Jake." And it was strange, since Jake and Zack weren't exactly best friends.

Lila shrugged. Like why on earth does that matter? And I was thinking, yeah, who cares. Just then I remembered Jake calling Zack, and Zack saying, "He knows it's us."

"Jake knew what was going on," I said, thinking out loud. I was wondering how, when I figured it out. "Someone put up one of those security cameras at my house. I saw it when Greg and Zack grabbed me. It had to be Jake." And I was pissed, because, Jake could've told my dad what was going on, but he didn't. Yeah, he wouldn't want to be the one to get Greg and Zack in trouble. And he wouldn't want to tell how he knew.

"OK, that's creepy," Lila said, but she was still waiting for her phone. She really wanted to go.

Then it hit me. "Maddy turned around in my driveway! If the camera got her car, and Jake had the video, someone might believe me!"

Lila looked stunned. Like, all of a sudden, there was a chance I was not lying.

"Yeah," I said. "I've been telling the truth." "Oh, my God! Jimmy! Call him!"

I grabbed her phone and I was about to call when I stopped. I was thinking furiously. The number of missed calls probably meant Jake didn't know about Greg yet. "The second Jake finds out about Greg, he was gonna freak. He'd get rid of the video so no one would think he was any part of what happened or knew anything about it."

Lila nodded, she had started to get it.

I looked around and saw Dave Perez was preparing to go live. "And Jake's just about to find out," I said.

My only hope was to get to Jake's house and grab his computer. Jake's house was three blocks away. I saw Deputy Baker pulling out handcuffs. If I didn't go now, it would be over.

"I've got to get to Jake's," I told Lila.

"You can't," said Lila. "Everybody's watching you." "Just distract them. Please."

Lila's eyes widened. Then she nodded. She took a deep breath, then she started yelling and running toward the TV crew. Everyone turned to stare at her.

I took off and didn't look back. About 50 seconds later, I heard Deputy Baker yelling, "HEY! YOU! O'KEEFE!"

Like he expected me to stop. I didn't, I kept running like hell. Then everyone started running after me.

I knew the deputies were gonna go back for their cars any second, so I cut through a couple of backyards and went through to the next street. I was hoping I would lose them, but I didn't. One of them was right behind me and gaining. I was about a block away from Jake's when I thought, maybe this was too dangerous. But then I remembered Maddy and kept going.

I got to Jake's and banged on the front door as hard as I could. I was panting so bad I couldn't even answer when someone asked who it was. The deputy was just steps behind when Jake's mom opened the door. I didn't say anything as I pushed past her and started running up the stairs. As she was standing there all shocked, the deputy ran in right after me.

I burst into Jake's room and he stared at me, stunned. He was on his laptop and I saw the video of my house.

"Don't delete it!" I screamed. Except that was exactly what Jake was about to do, but the deputy charged in with his gun drawn and yelled, "HANDS IN THE AIR! BOTH OF YOU!"

CHAPTER TWENTY-FIVE

It took several days to sort things out. Deputy Baker didn't want to admit he was wrong at first. But when the cops and the attorneys and everyone saw Jake's video, they knew Maddy was lying. They knew she wasn't where she said she was. They kept asking her questions, and, finally, she didn't have any answers.

Mr. Larsen got hold of the tape where Deputy Baker talked to Maddy after my dad reported me missing. Mr. Larsen asked if I wanted to see it. After I thought about it, I said OK.

The tape was in black and white and the quality was terrible, but it was the creepiest thing I had ever seen in my life. Maddy was sitting at this table and Deputy Baker was sitting across from her and he was hanging on her every word.

The tape began with Maddy saying, "It was an accident." And Deputy Baker repeated, "An accident?"

Then Maddy said, "I mean, if you want to say it was someone's fault, I guess it was Jimmy's fault."

Deputy Baker nodded, like that was what he wanted to hear.

Seeing that Deputy Baker was already on her side, Maddy got all chatty. "Jimmy was a freak, but I'd talk to him sometimes. I mean, he hated his life and I hated mine. Then I told him I wanted to run away from home, but I didn't have any money. He said he'd give me five hundred dollars if I did something. And I thought, wow, that would totally be enough."

Deputy Baker said, "Five hundred dollars," and Maddy nodded, "Yeah."

That was when Deputy Baker brought out cigarettes and offered one to Maddy. She was being interrogated and he was giving her a cigarette. "Smoke?" he asked, and Maddy grinned, "Sure."

Deputy Baker lighted two cigarettes and handed her one. As they smoked, Deputy Baker asked, "And what were you supposed to do for five hundred dollars?"

Maddy said, "Make Joe stop bothering Jimmy." Then she smiled really seductively and said, "Know what I mean?" And, even though the tape was black and white, you could practically see Deputy Baker blushing.

Then Maddy said, "So, I met Joe at the game and we, like, went in his car. But, afterwards, Joe was still mad because Jimmy got him in trouble with his dad. And Joe had this - this thing of gasoline - so he opened it to show off and said he was gonna throw it at Jimmy's house and scare him. Meanwhile, I was thinking, shit, now Jimmy's not gonna give me the money. So, I grabbed Joe's wallet to see if he had money, but he didn't. Then I got mad and I threw it out the car window. Joe kicked me out of the car and told me he won't let me back in until I found it. But then, it was dark and I couldn't see his stupid wallet. So, I said, turn on the damn lights. He started the car, and suddenly, his whole car exploded! I freaked out and left. No one but Jimmy knew it was me."

In the tape, Deputy Baker was just staring at her. It was almost funny, except it was so scary that he believed her. Finally, Deputy Baker cleared his throat and thought of one good question. "If it was an accident, why would Jimmy O'Keefe make up this story?"

But Maddy was way ahead of him. "Jimmy was afraid if Joe's friends found out, they'd blame him and beat him up bad. And, even if it was an accident, he thought he'd still get in trouble. So, he said, if I told anyone, he'd say I did it on purpose and he'd deny he ever agreed to anything. Only I got more and more scared, what if someone figured out it was me? So, today, Jimmy was at my house and I said, I'm telling. Jimmy just wanted to go to the police first."

"And if Jimmy said you started the fire at Joe's house tonight?"

Maddy looked him right in the eye and said, "He'd be lying. I never left my neighbor's house. You were there, you know that. Jimmy O'Keefe's lying."

Deputy Baker nodded like he was convinced, and then the tape ended right there.

Mr. Larsen played the tape one more time, and, after he did, he looked shaken. I guess he had never seen someone lie the way Maddy did. Then he said, "It was lucky you got the video from your friend." By my friend, he meant Jake. And it was lucky because Jake admitted, if the deputy hadn't screamed at him to throw his hands in the air that second, he would have deleted it.

"Because if you didn't," Mr. Larsen said, "I don't think I could have saved you." But Mr. Larsen did end up saving me. The deputy district attorney, this real tough woman, wanted to charge me with breaking and entering, because, I had to admit I broke into Maddy's house. Mr. Larsen had to point out that they were gonna need me to testify against Maddy. And he was not going to let me testify without a deal. So, finally, he worked it so I got six months of community service and, if I complete it, the whole thing gets expunged, which means, wiped out.

In court, I had to explain everything just the way it happened: what Maddy did to Joe and Greg and what she tried to do to me. Maddy's lawyer decided he better get her to change her plea, and, part of it was, Maddy had to admit everything. She was gonna be in prison for, like, forever.

Nothing too bad happened to Zack. I kind of said all the creepy stuff was Greg, so Zack knew he owed me. And Jake convinced everybody he deserved the reward. After what Mr. Larsen said about Jake's video saving my life, I was OK with that.

My dad was so glad it was over.

CHAPTER TWENTY-SIX

I was back at school and everyone just wanted to forget about what happened. They didn't come out to say they wanted to forget about it, but that was what they meant when they said it was time to "move on" and "put all this behind us" and all that crap. Like, if you didn't pay attention to something, that was supposed to make it go away. That just ensured the problem wouldn't go away. You needed to think about stuff and try to figure it out, or you'd go crazy.

I spent a lot of time thinking about what happened to me. I mean, I figured I got picked on because dudes thought they could get away with it. And they do, if you don't stand up to them.

That's why I'm telling you, don't take shit from anyone. Ever. Hiding in the library? No. Pretending you didn't get beat up when you did? No. You're gonna feel a whole lot better if you fight back. Or tell someone. And if the person you tell doesn't believe you, tell someone else. And don't take it personal. Because if someone is so screwed up he needs to hurt you, it's not even about you.

I read about this one school that had a 'safe room,' and if a dude was being picked on, he was supposed to go there so he could feel safe. I think that's about the worst idea ever. Everyone's gonna know you're in there, so it's like wearing a sign saying, "Hey, I'm being bullied." That's gonna thrill the dude messing with you. And it sure as hell won't make him stop.

So, if it was up to me? I'd put the bullies in a room. I'd have this one big old room and I'd take every bully from every school around and I'd shove all of them in this one big room all together. The room would have to be as big as an airplane hangar or maybe five airplane hangars. I wouldn't let them out until they promised they were gonna stop hurting other dudes. They'd promise, and they'd come out one by one. On account of, there'd always be someone meaner in that room. And, mostly, they'd all be scared shitless because bullies are always cowards. Always.

• *Thank you again for purchasing this book. Author's name is Stephen Uzoma Obinna. I hope you enjoyed it. If you did, be kind to leave me a review. You will find the book, if you search for my name and the title on Google (Stephen Uzoma Obinna). Thank you so much.*

Printed in the United States
By Bookmasters